STRINGS

Ruthanne Reid

4th Floor Publication
MESA, AZ

Ruthanne Reid/4th Floor Publication
www.AmongTheMythos.com

Publisher's Note: This is a work of fiction. Names, characters, places, and incidents are a product of the author's imagination. Locales and public names are sometimes used for atmospheric purposes. Any resemblance to actual people, living or dead, or to businesses, companies, events, institutions, or locales is completely coincidental.

Book Layout ©2013 BookDesignTemplates.com

Ordering Information:
Quantity sales. Special discounts are available on quantity purchases by corporations, associations, and others. For details, contact the "Special Sales Department" at the address above.

Strings/ Ruthanne Reid.—1st ed.
ISBN: 978-0-9852600-5-7

To Cameron, Nikki, and Kelli
Dargons rule.

"Men heap together the mistakes of their lives, and create a monster they call Destiny."

–JOHN OLIVER HOBBES

1 AN ELF IN MANHATTAN

My music made a lovely magic. It was tiny magic, sure, but effective: it thickened the air and deepened the candles' warm light, caressed the listener like intimate fingertips and teased sleeping nerve-endings toward a gently quivering wakefulness.

Go, me. I made it all happen.

Generally speaking, humans suck at love. They go into it selfishly, thinking of themselves and not the needs of the other, already planning in their little heads what they'll do when it doesn't work out. Idiots. Does anything else work that way? Can you learn art or become a mechanic without devoting yourself to those crafts? Can you graduate from college without paying attention to a coursework's needs, without being willing to spend time feeding it what it requires?

Well, yes, you can, but not *well*. And yes, colleges have needs, too. Every living thing does.

I could help the lovelorn attendees of tonight's bar-hop, and I had every reason to. Helping them helped me. The more they loved, the more I fed—and while humans do suck at getting love started, once it takes root in them, it grows like Kudzu. (That Kudzu-thing was one of my cousin's ideas, by the way. Don't look at *me*. I'm not a plant-wizard.)

My set was nearly done, which meant it was time to build up to my exit. Step one: a Spanish riff with a hint of blues, tossing in just enough Elvis to bring out the smiles, because smiles make everybody see the beauty of their partner. It's magic!

Step two: sadder arpeggios, delicately plucked, as if the strings sang only when tears fell upon them. The fragility of life and its shortness (short for humans, that is; there's a reason we call you lot the Ever-Dying) sank in like a stain, and all my listeners knew it. They knew they didn't have much time, knew that things might change, knew that they could lose this special other person to the inevitability of the grave.

I'd never leave them there, of course. It was time for step three: *hope*. Trills in a faster pace with high, quick chords danced from my fingertips like sun-sparkles on water. Yes, you lonely sods, you have each other now. No, that special person isn't perfect, but neither are you, and they will love you in spite of yourself. You could make each other happy. You could make this work—if you're willing to learn, to try, to forgive.

To love.

The magic moment bloomed, and love in the room tasted like raspberries in wine, toasted coconut and rum, and a hint of orange-infused chocolate. I could have stopped playing there, but I'm a thoughtful lover myself, don't you know, and the after-party is just as fun as the build-up. Tiny melodies trickled from my strings like secret giggles, bringing everyone gently down and getting them sleepily, drunkenly ready for bed.

See? I'm not a bad guy. I'm really not. Nobody among the Mythos would agree, but that's why I was there in the human

Ever-Dying world and not among my own kind. My world wasn't nearly as forgiving as this one.

At last, it was time to put the guitar away. The band for the next set was already bringing in their amps. For a fancy midtown Manhattan night-spot, it was almost peaceful. Quiet conversations glittered with intimate and precious words, requiring little volume. Yum, yum, yum. Delicious.

All right, so I know it probably horrifies you that I do this. It's manipulation of the highest form (which *some* would call art), and flirts with the concept of non-consent and force. Well, I'm not forcing anyone. *Encouraging* silly people to do things they should be doing anyway is very gray territory, but I'm all about gray territory. It's even in my name.

My view in the bar's huge mirror was a good one that night. I am of the Fey, Unseelie and royal, in fact, with perfect ears like long thin leaves and enough magic to keep them hidden. My spun-gold hair (which I do *not* hide) falls just past my shoulders, and though I'm lovely enough to be a woman (if I do say so myself), my strong jaw and my cheekbones preclude that misconception.

I'm distinctly male, yet fabulous. Take that, Orlando Bloom.

I'm just glad Tolkien finally broke the world of the stupid idea that elves are all tiny and annoying. Those are not elves. Those are sprites. It's thanks to all that sprite nonsense that the word "elf" has become offensive.

"Hey, Grey. Can we get you to fill in Friday?"

This manager wasn't interesting because he loved nobody, and that made him taste like dusty cement. The paycheck he handed me, atoned for much. Nice. "Sorry, but no. I'm booked through March."

He laughed and made some remark about schedules, his ex-wife, and their broken children, and I didn't bother to tell him I probably wouldn't be back to his bar ever again. Crazy Ever-Dying humans, always wasting the short time they have. Makes me sick.

I sighed a hefty sigh as I slid my guitar into my hatchback. On the front passenger side lay a wide-brimmed hat, a bolo tie, and a leather thong for tying back my hair, all prepped for the country-western bar that was my next stop. The cowboy boots were new, and kind of stiff, so—

There was a blue envelope lay on my dashboard.

I had not put a blue envelope there. Someone or something had been inside my car!

Rage made me briefly stupid. How dare they, whoever they were! This was just rude. Ah, but only another magic-user could have gotten through my little wards, and if I'd been thinking clearly, I'd have abandoned the car, the clothes, and the lot, and run for the proverbial hills. Instead, I snatched up the offending stationary with all due drama, and only then saw what was written on the front.

It bore my full name in thin, flowing handwriting perfect enough to come from a laser printer: ***John Baron Grey***.

I knew this handwriting. Only one person would come to me this way, with easy knowledge of where I was and who I was, and leave just a simple note without any traps set or warning flares placed. No wards I could put up would have stopped him, anyway.

I didn't know what he wanted, but I already owed him more than I could ever repay. My love-high went out like a candle in a stiff breeze. His persistence in thinking I'm a better person than I am always holds me like a vice.

I keep forgetting you're human, Ever-Dying. You have no idea who I'm talking about, do you?

Notte is... What terms shall I use? Ancient? Magical? Unique? Glorious beyond all reason, in spite of his disturbing penchant for blue velvet and formal dinner parties?

He's soft-spoken. He's deeply powerful. He's the nicest man I've ever met, and he scares most among the Mythos to death because he can do something we don't understand: he can turn humans into *us*.

You don't get it. People are magical among the Mythos, or they're Ever-dying. You're born magical or you're not, and *humans are not*.

Before you go off on witches and ghost-hunters and special sparkly New Age angels, hear me out. Bats have sonar. Eels have electricity. We have magic. You don't. Yet Notte can take an ordinary human and transform her into something else. She becomes like him, never-aging, requiring a specific and sticky substance to live, and like him, can change other human beings the same way.

Yes, it's like a disease, and no, I'm not being nice about this, and yes, he is my friend, but I'm not nice when I'm hungry. When I'm hungry, my Unseelie nature comes out. We are not a nice people.

I was hungry, and I couldn't bring myself to open the envelope. After the next gig, I'd open it. Not before. Notte would understand still being hungry. Of all those among the Mythos, he definitely could not blame me for that.

2 CATCHING UP TO YOU

My next gig went to crap.

The bar was dry as a bone. Nobody was in love, everybody was drunk, and I felt like I was licking the inside of an empty soup-bowl. I could smell what had been in there, but nothing was left for me. My chords tripped clumsily over their own bar-lines, and I even hit two wrong notes. Me! Wrong notes!

The surly bartender had checked out completely, drying the same glass for the past fifteen minutes. It's a safe bet he wished he had somewhere else to be. Or maybe he just wished he had more hair. That look could have covered either, truthfully.

Soon, the only people left in the bar were six middle-aged ladies, tipsy enough to giggle and glance my way speculatively before giggling some more. They gave the impression of old friends who go out regularly, without a chance of romance. At least they liked how I look. At least *somebody* was having some fun.

Bored Fey means mischievous Fey, yeah? It was time to be ridiculous. "Oh, here, upon a weeknight dreary, thus I played for bleak and beery humans dancing quaint (but ancient!) steps to my well-practiced lure," I crooned, following it with a bunch of pointless *oooohs*.

At least one of them was literate and whispered to the others. They all gave me their attention.

I winked salaciously at them. "While I drank them, my lust capping, suddenly there came a tapping as of someone gently rapping, rapping at the pub's front door. 'Tis some poor drunk oaf,' I muttered, 'tapping at the pub's front door—only this, and nothing more.'"

None of it fit into the standard meter, but the ladies were too tipsy to care, and now I was entertaining myself. I stood and raised one boot to rest on the stool to give the world a good look at my *business*. "Ah, distinctly I remember, it was in the bleak December, and each separate belching singer left his mark upon the floor. Naturally, I mean the bathroom—nasty place, I won't deny you—which could do with scrubbing nightly, scrubbing done upon the floor." Poe or any other poet would shriek and run at me with torches for that, but *carpe diem*, yeah?

By then, the ladies were laughing like teenagers while the bartender glared stormily in my direction. My new game of rude-but-handsome-country-singer was simply too charming to abandon, so I winked at them again, this time adding the kind of upside-down chummy nod that ladies find charming. "Land o' Goshen, they won't thank me! Called them out, embarrassed now, but at least I'm not a bore. Yes, that is true: I'm not a bore." I inhaled, ready to riff on the bar's reflections on the ceiling (which *could* have come from the bartender's head), when there came a tapping, gently rapping, rapping at the bar's front door.

Actually, that's a lie. The rapping wasn't gentle. It sounded like someone outside hammering with both fists, like they had to have a drink *right now* or die.

This was a bar. A public place. Open for four more hours, in point of fact. Why would anyone knock on the door of a bar?

The bartender scowled harder and put down his rag, then reached under the counter as if going for a weapon.

Well, that was interesting, but whatever was going on, I was hungry and tired, and needed to go someplace else. "Well, I thank all y'all for your kindness tonight," I drawled, my good-old-boy persona wrapped around me like a cloak. "I sure do enjoy playing for you, and I hope you can come back and see me again in March. Check my website for my full performance schedule. Be safe out there while you scamper on home!"

The ladies in the corner gave me a wild ovation, whooping and hollering, which might be why they didn't notice what the bartender did next. Whoever was outside pounded on the door again, hard enough to spill a little plaster dust from above, and the bartender evidently took that personally. He emerged from behind the bar with a thick wooden bat in his hands and marched for the door with murder in his eyes.

Whatever *that* was about, it was clearly time to leave, so I packed up my equipment maybe a hair faster than a human could manage. My only patrons were buzzed, anyway, so they didn't care. Guitar stowed, amp hefted, I headed for the back door, away from whatever was about to go down.

I wish I'd packed more quickly.

A storm of claws and black, shiny whips exploded through the door with a weird hiss like sand on glass, spraying splinters and glass everywhere. The ladies' screams sounded like the kind of things monsters like to wetly choke off. Self-preservation not being one of my weaknesses, I dropped everything and dove into the bathroom.

The bartender roared and apparently went to work with his bat. Meaty *whuds* like some kind of steak-tenderizing factory told me things were afoot, and I eyed the tiny window. Nope, couldn't fit through that, so I'd have to go back into the hall.

The ladies' screams grew closer. They weren't dead yet? What kind of self-respecting monster was this? I peeked out just as the six of them stumbled unsteadily by in their dress shoes, so frightened they kept running into the walls.

They had no shadows.

Let me say that again: they had no shadows.

I reacted without thinking, following them to the fire exit door because I had to prove my eyes wrong. And the moment they went through, they started *flaking*, like cold ash the morning after a fire. I skidded to a halt. One of them realized her arm was gone and screamed. Another fell into the trash cans because her face flaked away and she couldn't see anymore, and then they were all on the sidewalk, screaming while white ash drifted away like lazy fireflies.

The fire door swung closed in my face, and I dared not push it open. I didn't know if whatever had killed those women was contagious. I didn't know if everyone in the building was cursed. All I knew was their deaths had been activated when they stepped into the alley, and I didn't want to go the same way.

I started to go back to the bathroom, but the thought of being trapped in there with that monster coming for me was too much. Judging by the sounds from the main room, the bartender was still alive. Call me a fool, but I had to see.

What a sight he was.

He crouched on top of the thing, whacking it over and over with his bat. Sweat flew like Holy Water at a Mass. He clung to one of its tentacles with white-knuckled intensity, somehow keeping his feet when it rolled to try to crush him. Long, shiny whip-things flailed all around his head, trying to get him, but the beastie could only bend its limbs backwards so far, and he avoided them.

I didn't want to help. I doubted I even could. I've never liked violence that wasn't quick and close-up and secret, and this dark creature had *eats pretty silver-tongued Fey for breakfast* written all over it.

The bathroom, I thought. *I'm going to hide there. Forever. That stall on the left, that one will be my new home—*

And then the bartender spoke. "Set it on fire!" He brought the bat down with a meaty, wet thud and dodged a tentacle. "Fire! Set it on fire!"

Why not? I didn't know what this thing was, but most beings hate to be on fire, unless they happened to be made of it. "'Tis the season!" I howled for some idiot reason, grabbed a bottle of brandy, and threw it.

The monster was so rubbery the bottle bounced off, then happily smashed into the wall and splashed it anyway. I waved my hand, gathering the tiny flames from the candles on the tables, and blew a kiss to send them into the spill.

The brandy ignited.

Bright fire raced up the wall and over the monster, and the bartender jumped free as the blaze wrapped over the thing like new skin. The monster didn't shriek. It hissed, rattling like it had a throat full of rain-sticks under layers of rubbery flesh. When the bartender came running my way, I took the hint and vamoosed back down the hall.

Could we even go outside? I stepped back so he could be my guinea pig, to see if he would flake away, but I didn't get the chance. With a look that pronounced me a fool, he grabbed my arm and yanked me into the alley.

"Stupid elf!" he snapped, which was deeply insulting, but I was too busy to respond, what with running and panicking and sliding my hands over myself to be sure I wasn't flaking away.

I still had my shadow in the early-morning light. So did he. Maybe we were all right.

He took a sharp left and dragged me down the street, and we made another left around the next corner. That way, we put a full block behind us before the bar blew up.

Boom.

3 SHADOW-EATERS

The thing about explosions is it's not the *boom* that kills you.

First, there's a blast of heat and pressure (and, if you're too close, shrapnel), which compresses you. Organs, veins, and bodies in general don't like that. In the wake of that nastiness comes a split-second of vacuum, and for that instant, you are practically in space. Bodies don't like that, either, but don't worry: the final phase of an explosion fixes the vacuum bit. Pressure and air rush to fill it in with such force that you are thrown off your feet and into solid walls.

Bodies don't like *any* of this. It's a wonder anyone survives.

The bald barman and I made it far enough that we missed the worst of it, but the concussion still knocked us off our feet. I went flying into his back with far less grace than any Fey has a right to show. Broken glass rained down on us, which felt *terrible*, and the fire hydrant across the street blew with an ear-splitting clang and drenched everything.

I lay there on top of him like an idiot, just breathing. My ears rang, and my eyes felt squeezed. And I was very, very wet. Stupid fire hydrant.

Sirens rose and fell in the distance. I couldn't tell how close they were. I felt like a thousand needles stuck just inside my skin, but wriggling would not make them fall out—that's not how glass works—and I didn't have enough magic on-hand to fix it. My coffers were close to empty. I'd used too much in the last few months on dragons and girls and weirdness.

"Get off me," the bartender said to the sidewalk.

I rolled off him really, really carefully. There was glass in my hair. My hair!

He looked pretty bruised, too, and as he sat up, I finally got a good look at him. Beefy arms, old tattoos. Truly bald, as it turned out—it didn't look like he shaved his head. He had a paunch (at least my by standards, but mine standards are Fey. For an Ever-Dying human, I suppose he wasn't actually paunch-esque), and his white shirt and white apron were badly stained. He scowled at me. "You aren't safe."

"I'm not safe? *I'm* not? Who just blew up a monster in the middle of Manhattan?" I said, hopefully not too loudly. My ears rang, so it wasn't easy to tell. "The Mythos will be all over us! It'll be on the human news! What were you thinking?"

He took my tirade with unsatisfying calm. "I was thinking if it didn't die, everybody else would," he said, his voice rough and a bit breathless, and he stood. I say *stood,* but I really mean *pulled himself up the brick wall and leaned there, panting.* "And the Mythos can bite me."

I wanted to laugh. "That's a nice sentiment, but it rarely works out for the better. Trust me. I know from whence I speak." Awkward pause. "Well. Bye."

"Don't go. They'll get you."

I made a face at him. "They?"

"There are more of those things out there," he said, though he didn't actually say "things." He said something that rhymes with muckers, but I promised I'd make this safe for your tender ears, so. "They all know about you." He wiped his face with his sleeve, making both a little dirtier. "They're connected. They know you got away. If you leave, they'll hunt you down and get you."

Oh.

Well, shit.

Ever-dying humans panicked all around us, running away from danger to save themselves, or toward it to help others. So many sirens... we might as well have been in the middle of a war zone, and that damned hydrant was still shooting into the air, raining on everybody.

Dammit. *Dammit.*

You know what happened to me three months ago? I had a run-in with dragons and prophecies and magnificent damsels, and at the end of everything, I'd been warned. I'd been warned something was going to happen here, and I hadn't listened. Dammit. "Explain," I commanded, levelling my finger in the bartender's face.

"Yeah. Okay. Come with me. We'll tell you everything." He pushed off the wall, a little unsteady, and limped away from the chaos.

"There's a 'we,' now? Who's we? Do you belong to a coalition of bartenders for justice?"

He ignored me and looked for a taxi. I confess, I did, too. My precious guitar was gone, I had glass all over me, and I'd felt better. I lacked the courage to look at my face in any reflection. If it was cut, I didn't want to know.

What do you call a group of bartenders, anyway? A highball? A blend? A garnish? "Hey, Baldy."

"My name is Barry." He scowled at the passing fire truck.

Bald Barry the Bartender. You can't make this stuff up. "We need healing before we go anywhere. I'm cut. You probably have at least one broken thing in that pitiful human body of yours. If you're nice, I might see my way to helping you instead of letting you languish with punctured lungs or bladders or testes."

His eye twitched. "I forgot how annoying elves were."

At least this horrible situation could be a little more fun if he could verbally spar. "This annoying Fey knows a healer six blocks north of here. And 'elf' is offensive."

He grunted.

Six blocks was a long way to limp, but taxis had gone extinct in the middle of this. Barry made a pained face, but didn't complain. We pushed ourselves and got there in just over an hour of bleeding, grumpy silence.

<hr />

The healer I knew was a crotchety old bitch—sorry, *harridan*—but she took American money in payment, and was good enough at what she did.

I won't dwell on the experience. Her guise was "human fortune teller," and she was so 1950's-over-the-top it was embarrassing to even be seen in the place. Vibrant scarves, enormous jewelry, long black curls and violently red lips, and an atrocious accent all complimented incense strong enough to choke a horse.

As for what she really was, let's just say the combination of djinn and rusalka produces dark and hungry creatures, but at least they're good at healing.

"Thank you," Barry said with far more sincerity than he offered me, and she smiled and cooed and blushed at him and offered her hand. Somehow, he found a spot to kiss between all the rings and bangles.

He was flirting. While I was being hunted. The *nerve.*

She looked at me, and her pupils went cat-slitted and her smile turned real. "You are welcome here, silver-tongue. I will make you very happy if you stay with me."

I'd be *happy* until she sucked the last drop of life out of me, no doubt. "There will be no silver-tongued snacking tonight," I said, and turned to Barry. "My shirt is ruined. My hair is a mess. I smell like Nag Champa. We're leaving."

Rosa laughed and waggled her fingers after us as I dragged Barry away.

⊚≫≪⊚

I calmed down a bit by the time we reached his destination.

Barry (or some member of his mysterious "we") lived in a luxurious pre-Depression building in the upper West Side. Polished-wood cherubs hung over the lintels, reflected in salmon-colored marble floors that gleamed as if just polished. The elevator doors were shining brass, engraved with dragons and Latin phrases and with nary a fingerprint to be seen.

The Latin on those doors said *Fronta Nulla Fides,* which means *place no trust in appearances.* Well, that wasn't ominous at all!

"This is a nice place," said Barry. "I gotta introduce you, or they won't let you in."

Posh. No, really.

I studied the stained glass windows as he introduced me, telling the doormen I was George his cousin, which earned a double-take as the only resemblance Barry and I shared was a Y chromosome. The doorman wrote it all down anyway and tapped on the little monitor to his left, subtly inset in the marble wall.

"George? Really?" I said under my breath as we approached the elevator, which (of course) was paneled in mahogany.

"First name I thought of," he said.

"Being your cousin was bad enough, but George? What an absurd choice."

"Quit it. Hey, Enrique!" he greeted the elevator man with enthusiasm.

I am not a *George*. Nevertheless, now was not the time to argue this overwhelmingly valid point.

We stepped out onto the seventh floor and into a private elevator foyer. An old, solid door, complete with burnished brass knob, stood between us and Barry's bartender-coalition.

He hesitated, hand on the knob. "Be nice. They don't know nothing. Not really."

"I'm always nice, you cad." I waved my hand.

He may have rolled his eyes as he turned the knob.

We walked into an actual gallery with parquet flooring, ghastly black and white wall-art, and stark white armchairs on either side of a pointlessly shallow table. To our right stood a jade fu-dog, hollowed out for umbrellas, and a small table of black marble with inlaid mother-of-pearl in the pattern of a peacock.

I whistled. "Hell of a place you have here, Barry."

Barry dropped his keys on the peacock-table. "We don't got time for foolishness." He marched to the right.

It was a dining room, judging by the long, burled-wood table, though the people seated around it didn't look like bartenders to me. "Barry!" A young woman in short-shorts and a halter-top leaped to her feet, then froze, staring at me.

The group all looked back and forth between us, then concentrated on the familiar.

"What happened? You okay, man?" said a middle-aged man in army pants and a white t-shirt. His muscles bulged beneath his dark skin, veins visible, like he'd been doing pull-ups to pass the time until our arrival.

I took stock of the other three, who all stared at me as if my very appearance had switched off their brains: two young male teenagers in jeans and beat-up band shirts, and an old man in a white pinstriped suit and white goatee.

"What is this?" said the old man, gesturing at me as if I were some vagabond.

"He's Fey," Barry said with no further introduction.

They stared harder.

Well, there was no harm in playing the part. Vaseline off the lens, as it were. I dropped my wards, and my beauty *shone.* My silver eyes slanted. Subtle light pulsed beneath my skin, as if shining from a distance, and my bone-structure sharpened. My glorious ears, long as my forearms and so thin the light shone through them, announced my pure Fey heritage.

"Fey?" said Pinstripe, as if insulted.

"Some call me Tim," I intoned.

None of them watched Monthy Python, apparently.

"His name's *Grey*," said Barry.

"You're not hurt?" demanded Pinstripe. He really looked like something out of the third Matrix movie, all neatly trimmed and arrogant.

Barry shrugged. "He took me to a healer. Was with me when it took the bait, though."

Eyes widened all around.

"So they're coming for him," breathed the shorter teen. "The shadow-eaters!"

I promptly laughed my head off.

I know I was being a dick, but I couldn't help it. Have you ever laughed at something folks around you find *very serious indeed?* It doesn't go well.

Various expressions of anger and fear came at me with wide eyes and rapid breathing, and the younger teen clenched his fists. "Stop it!"

I wiped my eyes as that awkward moment rolled past. "Shadow-eaters? Are you serious?"

"As death," said the old man.

That set me off all over again.

"They're real," Barry grunted.

I waved my hand. "No. No, they're not. They're stories, *literally* created to frighten Fey children into obedience. Who even told you that word?"

They all looked at Barry, which was a puzzling thing. He wasn't magical, but maybe he had Kin in his family, clinging to shreds of tales from its Fey heritage.

I shook my head. "Barry. Darling. Shadow-eaters aren't real."

They all gawked at me with such terror I almost felt sorry for them.

"They're real," said Pinstripe, and stroked his white beard. "You of all people should know the power of disbelief to protect those who do not wish to be seen."

Wait. What? "Excuse me?"

"You Mythos do that. Don't you? You stay out of sight, convincing us you're all lies and fairytales so we don't hunt you down like so many of you deserve to be hunted."

Well, *he* could just go to hell. "You don't know what you're talking about, old man."

He leaned forward, clearly used to being the authority in the room. "Isn't that the principle? Our disbelief keeps you safe because we don't look for you. Because we don't see you." He pointed at me. "Shadow-eaters are real. Whether you believe in them or not isn't going to change that, Fey."

Granted, shadow-eaters were very scary tales, and I'd seen some very scary things today, but this was absurd. This was like someone trying to tell you the thief you saw wasn't an ordinary thief, but was *actually* an alien, escaped from Area 51 and stealing purses to get by until the mother ship arrived. Complete bunk.

And that old man sounded like he knew... a lot. Far too much. I looked at Barry.

The bartender remained unreadable.

Great. *Someone* had been talking, and that meant if I hung around, those among the Mythos might assume that someone was me.

The old man looked at Barry. "Go with Cassie. Get checked out."

Barry shrugged and went with the short-shorts girl out of the room, leaving me with the troop of Ever-Dying know-it-alls.

I hadn't decided how to reply yet. Sarcasm was safe. "So what are you people supposed to be, eh? The committee for hunting Mother Goose and plucking her feathers?"

"Survivors," said the older teen, who had to be about seventeen. "We lived like you did. We're hunted like you are."

This had gone too far. "Listen to me. Shadow-eaters aren't real."

"They are. They got my parents. My sister." He looked away. "She was going to college on a scholarship."

And it went from laughable to maudlin, just like that. "It wasn't shadow-eaters."

"They got my whole class," said the younger teen, who was maybe fourteen. "All of us. They claimed it was a subway accident, but it wasn't."

"And my daughter," said the black man in the army-wear. "She was twelve."

"And my wife," said Pinstripe. "We're all survivors by the skin of our teeth, but by escaping, we're marked. Shadow-eaters bind themselves to your moorings, Fey. There's nowhere you can go to escape them."

Moorings? He knew about *moorings*? How much did these people know? "Moorings?" I tried, innocently.

"Don't play ignorant. Moorings bind the soul to the body. When all the moorings break, you die."

That's it. We were all screwed. "You know you shouldn't know any of this, right? That it's illegal? That we're all going to be drawn and quartered because you know these things?"

"What're you talking about?" said the older teen.

Pinstripe ignored him. "The shadow-eaters eat your moorings, all the way to your soul. They eat your taste, your memories, and then they spit you out empty, like a blank piece of paper. Your shadow disappears because light reacts to you differently. It's quantum physics."

It was quantum craziness, that's what it was. He was talking about real shadow-eaters as if they existed. As if that thing that I saw—

The women's shadows were gone.

No, this had to be nonsense. I turned to the older teen. "The things you're talking about are not general knowledge, and a lot of power and money and magic has been spent to keep them secret. If anyone important finds out you know these things, you'd be in trouble. Big trouble."

The teen looked ill. "Great. Effing great," he said (though he didn't say "effing," but you get the idea) and sat bonelessly.

Pinstripe shook his head. "It's moot. If the shadow-eaters devour us, your laws won't matter, and if we survive, we can handle your laws."

I covered my face and groaned. Bravado. It would be rousing if he were the hero of this story, but he wasn't, so. "No. No, you won't."

"We've killed three of them," he insisted. "Four, if Barry was successful today, that's beside the point. They're still coming for you. Join us."

And they all stared at me, waiting for something.

Waiting for what? To say I was sorry? To hoist an axe and shout *we'll get 'em, sarge?*

See, if this were a movie about a plucky band of adventurers, I'd be the idiot who wants to go off alone and get skewered. But it wasn't. It *wasn't* a movie, and it was *my* story, not theirs, and I wanted to strangle everybody.

I turned around and walked out. But not back to the elevator. I passed through the gallery to the room on the other side.

A proper living room, that, complete with a light Persian carpet the size of a small swimming pool and a real wood-burning fireplace. Museum-quality art larger than I was hung on the walls, and a grand piano overlooked Central Park. I opened a window (it had to be cranked open, for real), leaned out, and just breathed.

Did you ever have a thing that you were afraid of, a thing you were *taught* to fear, and everybody you knew held in true and visceral terror?

Did you then have to fight *not* to believe in it later when you were told it wasn't true? A thing you now had to pretended not to check for around corners and in closets. A thing you laughed off even though it still terrified you but shouldn't because *it wasn't real*, and only an idiot would continue fearing.

Not much like Santa Claus, yeah?

This is a shadow-eater: manipulation. Every Fey child lives in the fear of them, and only much later are we told it was a necessary lie to make us behave—which is sort of valid. Try controlling a magically empowered child without some form of manipulation. Just try.

These stories keep us close to our parents and stubbornly obedient, because if we were bad, the monsters would get us, because if we were bad, the shadow-eaters would *eat us*, and sure, it doesn't create a lot of ground for trust between parent and child later on, but what can you do? Everybody is dysfunctional in some way or another.

These monsters *couldn't* be shadow-eaters, of course, but Pinstripe said they'd marked me. That could be true; there are things that scent you and never let go, things that chase and hunt you for the rest of your life, until they end it or something else does. Black hounds. The Wild Hunt. *Things.* And what had I seen downtown today? Those women had no shadows, and they'd fallen apart to ash.

I sighed and hung my head, properly miserable. Someone on the street below looked back at me.

It was quite a distance—definitely enough to make it hard to differentiate one person from another, especially someone I'd only seen once in a beer-splashed hall. Yet there she was, one of the women from the alley who'd run by me and turned to ash, calmly staring. People flowed around her like water around a rock, and she didn't move, watching my window. Like she knew where I was. Where we all were. I pulled back, shaking just a little. If it were true—*if* it were—then shadow-eaters were real.

And I was being hunted.

4 NOTTE

I debated going for help. Merlin might be willing to lend me aid if his niece asked him... although now they were both busy protecting that baby dragon thing, so he might not be able. Or worse, maybe he *could* protect me, but his solution would include hiding in his tower with him to wait it out. No, thank you.

What else could I do? I could go home—ha! No, I really couldn't. That was out.

Who owed me favors? Lots of folks, but that was no good. Magic is a very precise force, and limited by species; not everyone can fight everything. If my acquaintances were as helpless as I, they would not thank me for drawing these creatures to them and damning us all together.

That settled it: my only help was a crew of Ever-Dying humans who most definitely would not be able to keep me alive.

Yes, I couldn't keep them alive, either, but surely you see I'm worth more?

Sorry. That was a selfish, terrible thing to say, but it was how I felt at that moment, and we're being honest, aren't we? We've all had our worst days, and this was a bad one for me.

So I had a group of the Ever-Dying to work with. Right. If we were going to survive this, I'd need to take the reins. It was time to show them what they'd signed up for.

There was no door to slam in the dining room, so I announced my return with magic.

I hummed as I entered, a creepy tune in time with my steps that sent blue power skittering over their skin to raise their hair like static electricity before it bites. My own hair floated around my face as if I stood over a vent, all shimmery and gossamer gold, and just for fun, I made the lights flicker off completely for the count of three.

"Do you really think I should join *you*?" I modulated my voice so it sounded like many voices all around the room. "Do you actually believe you can offer anything to me? You, the Ever-Dying, who age and fail merely by *sitting there*, who have no power of your own, who have no way even to save yourselves? Do you believe I should join you? Do you? Why should I help you, instead of leaving you here to be destroyed?"

They stared (the Ever-Dying usually do), all of them breathless and terrified, everybody's face going different colors. Well, almost all; Barry looked bored. Standing by the swinging door into the kitchen, he crossed his arms and glowered. But that was all right. I could allow him some boredom. Bored, bald Barry the bartender had had a longer day than I had.

"We... we...." Pinstripe tried to pull it back together.

I waved my hand. "Silence! You speak secrets of which you know nothing! You talk of the Mythos, of the soul and its workings, of the ineluctable power of magic, and yet you know nothing!" I gave an extra burst of power, and my hair flew up around me like in some exorcist movie, only so much prettier. "I am the only one here with the right to such damning knowledge, and more than this—*I am the one who holds your lives in my hands.* You, who speak of the Mythos with such contempt, are you now prepared to be judged by them?"

I might have overdone it a little, because the younger of the two teens started crying, and the girl Cassie looked like she was about to be sick. If she ralphed on the old man's suit, I'd have to give her a prize.

It was kind of a game, yes. I'm Fey. What do you want?

Besides, it didn't matter because Barry marched right over and yelled in my face. "Cut it out! We don't got time for this!"

Cut it out is not the standard response to phenomenal cosmic power.

What was I supposed to do? I could zap him, but I was bluffing - I didn't have that much power left, and now he'd ruined the theatricality of it all, anyway. I let my hair fall down around my shoulders and gave him a pout that would haunt him (I hoped) for the rest of his stupid mortal life. "You're no fun."

They all stared, mouths open. This was a show of a different kind now.

"Fun? Fun? You think this is fun?" Barry growled in dire bartender warning. "We don't got time for fun! Freaking stupid elf. Did you count us? Do it now!"

He called me an elf again, the stubborn bastard.

Far be it from me to obey. Then again, I'm smart, and I couldn't help but tote everybody up just because he'd made me think about it: the old man, camo-pants guy, Cassie, teen one and teen two, Barry, and me. Well. That made seven.

Seven. *Shit.* "Oh," I said.

"Yeah. 'Oh,'" said Barry, and he had the nerve to poke me in the chest with his finger. "We got to act now. Everybody knows you're a special snowflake. Now help us, or you'll be a dead snow-flake."

"You mixed your metaphors," I whined, because I had to say something.

"Seven?" said the younger teen, hurriedly wiping his face. "So?"

"Seven's a number of amplification," said Barry, finger still on my chest like I was a piece of paper that might fly away. "With us together like this, we're a homing beacon. They'll find us for sure, and they'll probably converge."

You could smell the adrenalin spike.

"Calm down, Barry," I said, and pushed at his accusing hand. It didn't move, so I pushed again. "It's not that bad."

"It is that bad. We're running out of time!" He got right in my face to yell that, so it was time to teach him a lesson.

I kissed him.

Poor Barry. He went leaping backwards like I'd burned him, rubbing his mouth almost violently. "Son of a bitch!"

I laughed, so help me. "Did you forget we among the Mythos tend to be omnivorous?"

"Son of a bitch!" He rubbed his mouth again.

My tenuous grasp on the room was restored. "All right, humans, listen up, because I won't repeat this. You do not know what you're dealing with. Not about the shadow-eaters or anything else." I tossed my hair. "Never mind that you're in such violation of the laws that you could all be carted off. I like life. I *like* it, and I am not going to throw it away due to your incompetence or anything else, you understand me?"

Barry still looked like I'd made him swallow bad milk. "Son of a bitch," he said again.

"What are you proposing, exactly?" said Pinstripe, trying to keep his voice steady.

Time to drop a bomb. "I saw one of the victims outside the building. Outside the window, just now, before I came back in here. A woman who'd turned to ash and died—there she was, looking up at me. They already know where we are."

Cassie curled in on herself, hiding her face in a ball of arms and legs. The younger teen started to hyperventilate.

The old man took a deep breath. "We are safe here."

Oh, this should be good. "Pardon?"

He sat up straighter. "This building was planned by men in the know, Unseelie. It was built with silver from the other side, and iron made with dragon's blood, and a dozen other things. They can't reach us here. As long as we're in this building, we are safe."

I rubbed my face. "No. No, that won't work. Even if some crazy old-timey architect did use blessed silver and dragon's blood—" which is possible; I've known some older structures on the east coast that do. "—it also used other things. There are always cracks in every seam. A really determined monster will wriggle through miles of plaster to get what it truly wants."

Pinstripe wasn't through. "We're not your enemies, and I do not believe you are ours. We are in this together, united by the monsters under our beds."

I rolled my eyes at that one. "It's not just the bed-bugs you need to worry about. Do you even know what laws you broke?"

"We didn't do nothing," said the taller teen, clenching his fists.

Aww, they're so cute when they're young and stupid. "Yes, you did. Do you think you're safe because you're young? Or American? That's not how this works. You're dealing with magical beings who live for centuries, occupying empires that last millennia. Do you know how short your lives are? Do you really think anybody cares about the teeny tiny laws of a country two hundred years old, a country that changes its own laws on a daily basis? Do you really think the temporary lives of the Ever-Dying, built and discarded with such ease, matter to us?"

His mouth worked, but nothing came out.

"Be gentler," Barry said softly.

Well... he was right. Children are still children. "The laws are in place for a reason. You aren't supposed to know any of the things Colonel Mustard over here has been teaching you, and if anyone who really cared found out, you'd all disappear."

"So are you saying you don't really care?" Cassie said.

Clever girl. "I'm saying you'll be sent to the other side, and that's all she wrote."

They looked confused and afraid for one glorious second.

"The other side isn't death. It's where the magic people live," said Barry, ruining my moment, *like always*. "It's where they ran off to when we humans grew too populous for their taste."

"Populous? I love your vocabulary, Barry-cakes," I said, and batted my eyelashes at him.

"It's basically another dimension," said Barry, ignoring me completely. "He means they'd take us to their world, where we'd have to make new lives, new families, new everything, and we'd never be able to come back."

He said it so accusingly! "Well, that's better than being dead, isn't it?" I flipped my hair over my shoulder. "It's about safety. It's like what your FBI might do if you knew lots of state secrets. Witness protection program."

"More like dumped-on-your-own program," said Barry.

"Would that work?" The younger teen looked around. "Would they... could the shadow-eaters follow us there?"

"Yes, of course they could," I snapped, but then I wondered. I had no idea what world these things had come from. The seven Peoples of the Earth (Fey being one of them) each have their own little niches, but that didn't answer my question. What realm did these beasties call home? How had they even gotten here? You couldn't just hop through worlds willy-nilly whenever you wished. It wasn't that simple. How did a herd of these things come to be in New York City?

"Oh," said the older teen, and looked away, his eyes all shiny.

That made me mad. See, this is exactly what I was trying to avoid—being locked in here with a bunch of fools, frightened fools, fools with feelings and lives they thought worth protecting, hoping they could win by the power of being underdogs. It doesn't work that way, real life *doesn't work that way*, and we were all going to die, and I knew it, and they knew it, and everybody stared at the floor and the table and then me and each other and nobody said anything at all.

And then the doorbell rang, and we all jumped out of our skins.

A modified version of Big Ben's chimes bonged through the cavernous apartment. I will never admit to yipping like a fox with his tail stepped on. But maybe I did cry out. I know my ears went down like a donkey's, which was pretty embarrassing in itself.

"Who's there?" the smaller teen shouted from his place at the table, as if that did any good.

Barry charged past me with the determination of an angry rhino. We couldn't see the door from where we were, but everybody leaned forward over the table to hear, craning in an unconscious imitation of small children at a puppet-show.

They all felt so young just then, so helpless. These were *people*, as much as I tried to marginalize them, as much as I tried to say they were short-lived and therefore pointless. My stomach roiled; my skin crawled; and so I abandoned them and followed Barry into the hall.

Barry threw open the door and stared.

"Please forgive my intrusion," said a honey-tenor tone. "I am looking for a friend of mine, who I believe has come to this place."

I knew that voice.

"Uh," said Barry.

I was under grave stress, and so I peeked around the door like a deranged puppet.

The contrast between these two men was ridiculous. Barry, in worn jeans and a plain white t-shirt, his black no-slip trainers and shiny-shaven head was a man of this era and area, through and through. While Notte....

He looks precisely he stepped out of a painting from the Romanticism period. He always wears a blue velvet suit, and it should be ridiculous, but he makes it magnificent. Enormous brown curls hang loosely around his face. His sharp jaw, full-lips, and thick-lashed eyes enhance this utter, solid elegance so engulfing that you feel that maybe *you're* the one in the wrong century.

And there is something about him that just isn't normal.

It's hard to pinpoint and impossible to define. He's different somehow, his build, his features, but he's beautiful and so you stare, *but something is not normal,* and it isn't until you realize how old he is and how the weight of his years darkens the room like blackout curtains that your scared subconscious whispers *he's primal* and *young when monsters roamed the world* and you are afraid, because you know, *you know you're a mouse* and he, with his poet's face and artist's fingers, might just decide to crunch your bones.

He waited patiently, a man from other eras, from every era, for Barry to find his tongue.

"You," said Barry, which was odd because it was as if he knew him.

"I fear our conversation is urgent," said Notte, who didn't seem to know Barry back.

"Okay," said Barry, which is one of those funny words that technically means, *yes, I agree,* but in casual conversation really denotes *I heard the words you said, but I don't accept them.*

"Is he available?" said Notte, like he wanted to go on a play-date.

"Uh," said Barry. "Gimme a minute. Sir. Okay?"

"Of course," said Notte, and evidently stepped back with such grace that it would have felt hopelessly rude *not* to shut the door.

Barry closed it politely, and then turned to stare at me. "The hell, Elf?" And I knew for certain: Barry recognized him.

"What?" I said.

"Who was that?" called Pinstripe, looking whiter than usual. "My... the spells on this place... they didn't even let me know he was coming."

"The wind probably let him in," I said, and didn't bother to elaborate because I was sick of this and didn't care if he was scared. "Look, Barry, he... he calls me a friend."

"The hell he does. How did *you*—" I wish I could express the way he said that word. "—get to be his friend?"

"What is going on here?" Pinstripe demanded, standing again with a *thock* of his cane. "Who was that? How did he come here? Did you invite him?"

"Notte goes where'er he wishes," said Barry weirdly, looking at me like he was trying to dissect me with the raw power of dislike. "And if the elf really is his friend—"

"Elf is offensive, I will have you know," I huffed.

Barry studied me. "If he really calls you friend, then he can help us."

"Well. Maybe." I shrugged, not looking at him. "I'm not family, Barry-cakes."

"Don't matter. He came here for you."

"Yes, well, I may have forgotten about a letter he left on my dashboard," I mumbled.

"Somebody explain something!" camo-pants demanded.

I threw my hands in the air. "Fine. Fine!" And I opened the door.

Notte smiled at me as though it were wonderful to wait in a narrow elevator foyer with nothing to look at but a forgotten, dusty Christmas tree. "John."

"It's Grey. I'm in trouble." I felt six pairs of eyes burn into me like lasers. "We're in trouble."

There was the slightest, slightest pause. I doubt anyone but me would have caught it, but I did.

"I agree," said Notte. "May I enter?"

No, he doesn't need permission. He was being polite, you Philistine.

"Please." I stepped aside.

He introduced himself, and so help them, everybody responded. You just do that with Notte. He bows, you bow, he gives his name, and you give yours. I walked away to get some tea, so I missed some of that nonsense.

"I will not take much of your time," he was saying as I came back.

"Are you... somebody?" said the younger teen (named Mario, as it turns out). "I mean, somebody important? You got power, man?"

"Some might say so," Notte said with such gravity that the kid was encouraged to talk more.

"Can you help us?"

"I will attempt to so. You are being hunted," Notte said to the room at large.

It was funny to watch them. They sat up straighter and tried not to fidget. Mario became aware (possibly for the first time) that he had dirt under his fingernails.

"We know that," snapped Pinstripe, whose name was Peterson. I had to give him points for bravery. "Of course we know that. You come in here, calm and you think you can just... of course we know that."

"They are not shadow-eaters," said Notte (I resisted the urge to point at Pintstripe and shout, *Ha!)*, "although they do, in fact, eat the soul's moorings. They may not be what you feared, but I fear they are worse. They are every inch as wicked as your child's mind could imagine, for they are the First War's leftovers. We call them slivers."

Slivers. Slivers!

I smacked myself on the forehead. Slivers! Why did I think of that! But wait, if they were slivers, then that meant gods.

And I was nearly empty. I didn't have the power to fight gods.

"First War?" said Cassie, eyeing me warily.

"The very first—at least, the first which took place outside of Heaven," Notte said.

These people were human. They had no chance against slivers. I might have, but not like this. Dear hell, what had I stumbled into?

"What are slivers?" said camo-pants, otherwise known as Sam.

"They are sentient pieces of deities which have been destroyed," said Notte.

They had no chance. Only I did, and I needed a lot more power if I was going to take on pieces of gods. I couldn't wait. "Um. Notte?"

"Yes, John?"

"I'm hungry."

They all stared at me.

"There's sandwiches," offered Mario after a moment.

"That ain't what he needs," said Barry grimly. I glared at him.

Notte stood. "I will continue in a moment. Would you pardon an interruption? Is there a musical instrument in this place?"

The old man gestured. "Piano. In the other room. Why?"

"If you will grant us ten minutes apart, I will be able to enhance Grey's magic. I fear he is in dire need of sustenance."

Lots of stares.

"Give 'em the time," said Barry. "Let him do it."

I never thought he'd be in my corner.

Pinstripe shook his head at the floor, then made a shooing motion at us. He looked like he'd aged twenty years.

I walked away from them all over parquet wood floors, past the inlaid marble-top table in the foyer and the jade fu-dog, and pondered dying. Padded over the Persian rug, past all the artwork and unused fireplace, and tried to imagine being eaten or absorbed or torn to pieces. If I failed, I would be. Fey are delicious.

Notte walked with me. His steps—in spite of fine Italian-leather shoes—were completely silent.

The grand piano looked like it hadn't been played for a while, but I hit middle C, and to my perfect ears (I'm Fey, and they ARE perfect) it sounded moderately in tune. I sat down.

He put his hand on my shoulder. "Do not fear."

"Right." Rested my fingers on the keys, but did not play.

"You are capable of doing this."

"You don't know that." I stroked the keys. Would this be the last piano I ever touched?

All right, now *I* was getting maudlin.

"I do. You will not be going alone."

"You're coming?"

"No."

I didn't want to hear anymore while I was weak. So I played instead.

If there's anything we who know Notte know, is that *he* knows love. And he knows loss. And I know how to conjure both.

The piano isn't as good as the guitar, of course—it's too big, too orchestral, not intimate like the sound and sense of the tips of fingers and thin, rough string. Instead of whispers, it gave me rumbling bass like underwater currents, rushing against gravity toward treble melodies that sparkled like sun-lit puddles after the rain.

Softly, wordlessly, I began to sing.

Octaves rang like hammers on steel, and light arpeggios hinted at harps played in grand halls. And my wordless tune—I didn't bother with lyrics because I *made* all the meaning I needed— hung between them with a steady walking-tempo of simple range to counterbalance all the chords and chaos.

Minor key. Up and down, a slow melody with a quick under-rhythm, my voice a single perfect petal swept downstream. I didn't create this sound and song to make anybody fall in love. I did it to bring his love back to the surface.

And all his vast experience, all the love he'd ever generated, filled this room and me with a power and mourning so sweet that I wept as I played.

Can you feel sick while feasting? Can you know guilt even when being satiated on a level you barely believe is possible? His love poured out of him, overwhelming, drowning my hunger like a flood drowns a match, filling and surrounding and blinding me with all its power and passion and price.

Such price! The one he loves is dead, has been dead forever, will never return to him, and yet he *loves her so much* that there is no surcease, no break from his torment. He embraces it like he once embraced her, diving in and becoming one until he is carried by it instead of being crushed, and it tasted so good, and *he* tasted so good, and I felt nearly sick for using it to feed myself.

I stopped playing at some point, my hands still and fingers deep in the keys. I panted, and felt a little drunk. Woozy. Good, but definitely woozy.

"Thank you, my friend," Notte whispered, his hand on my shoulder and tears in his eyes.

I don't know why he thanked *me*. I was the one who'd benefited here. I felt like he should've hit me instead.

I'll tell you this, though: my magic was back to full power. Boy, was it: I hadn't been this full since I left home. At that very second, glutted on love so many centuries old I couldn't even consider it, I couldn't even feel afraid.

I did feel ashamed. Sometimes I see myself as a parasite, and wondered why I thought I have the right to live at all.

I'm Fey, so that shame wouldn't last forever. We're good at pushing off shame. *To* our shame.

I'm not very funny at all.

5 JUST A WANDERING MINSTREL, MA'AM

You're human, so you wouldn't know anything about the First War.

How can I emphasize the importance of this? All our history and education builds on it, echoes it, until every warp and weave among the Mythos follows its nautilus-spiral to narrow isolation.

Are you familiar with your Japan's Edo period? In an attempt to preserve its culture and prevent the influence of too much foreign policy and religion, Japan closed its borders and restricted trade. You're likely aware by now that the people of the Mythos do something similar: to protect ourselves, we stay away from *you.*

That's the royal "we," of course.

So here's what I was taught about the First War. One day, the Ever-Dying joined forces with powerful members of the Mythos in an attempt to take over the entire planet. And of course, since you people multiply like rabbits, even wiping out entire armies failed to stop you. Within a few short years, you'd be back, more numerous than ever and following the lead of some wicked and dangerous fool. With nothing more than time, numbers, and the power of the monster you followed, you humans nearly conquered us all.

This is what I was told. It's also a lie.

Here's what Notte told me instead.

The First War is the reason humans have the concept of "gods," as opposed to one great Creator. Those among the Mythos with a great desire for power tricked humans, took them, enslaved them, conscripted and used them like ammunition, a renewable and inexpensive resource. The end result was entire human cultures willing to sacrifice their own children to these so-called gods, and it was those gods who made war on the rest of us.

It took everything the Seven Peoples of the Earth had to end this takeover, and we suffered for it - the Guardians were decimated, the Sun scattered, the Darkness made weirder and more reclusive than ever. The Dream just *left*, permanently inhabiting the realm between worlds and so removing themselves from the equation. Even to us, they're like ghosts.

After it was done, we Fey tightened our borders and retreated. Our leaders were so desperate to maintain isolation that they created the Throne and the Scepter — sentient, powerful instruments that harness the magic of Seelie and Unseelie fey from birth. They choke it off, limit it, preventing us from revealing ourselves or getting any ideas; they funnel our extra magic to our rulers and protectors to keep us safe.

That's what we're told.

There's nothing quite like having the power you yourself generate being sucked out of you, leaving you empty. Forced to find other sources. To scavenge.

According to my teachers, the First War is why no other Peoples of the Earth can be trusted. We especially can't trust humans, since you never know when they'll sell themselves to somebody as weapons again. The First War is why the Fey will never allow the seven Peoples to unite again, lest they grow too strong and break the balance of power that gives us peace.

You heard me right. My people think we have the right to police everybody.

Why, yes, it *is* obviously biased toward Fey being everybody's keepers! Yes, it *does* make inter-species discussion rather difficult! Yes, it *is* the reason all our power is stolen from us at birth, channeled into the Throne and the Scepter, to be released as our benevolent rulers decree. Yes to all of that, and it's all based on the lie that we poor Fey were victimized, attacked, with no collective way to defend ourselves.

My teachers never said anything about the Fey joining in with the humans, being part of the rebellion, nearly overthrowing the rest of the world. I know now. Notte was *there*. His version of what happened is messier than I was told, but I believe him. We Fey sold ourselves out, too, following some monster's shiny song.

It's an unpopular truth, can you imagine? And you wonder why I don't like to go home.

To say the mood was awkward when we returned would be like saying the ocean is wet, or darkness is addicting, or Fey are pretty. All givens.

We walked back into a dining room filled with suspicious, angry stares, created by people who were not okay with this invasion, but far too tired to put up much protest. Their close-knit group had been invaded; and now, I was drunk.

I couldn't help it. Notte's love... intoxicating.

Together, we walked back into the dining room, he grim and I chipper, and I waved at everybody then sat after a series of powerful and possibly gravity-defying steps.

Glory, I felt wonderful. I think I was glowing. No, I *was* glowing: I could see the shadows of my long, thin ears against the tabletop.

"What's this? He's drugged? What did you do?" said Pinstripe, recoiling.

"His system is merely overwhelmed with an influx of power. He will find his balance shortly," said Notte, and read the room's mood. "I can see you have all been through so much. I am sorry."

"No, you're not. You don't know us," said camo-pants Sam.

He was wrong.

Notte bowed slightly, an acknowledgment without agreement, and when he looked up, his eyes held pain. "I have been the victim of gods' wrath and slivers' hunger. I have lost family. I am sorry for you, in a way few can be."

Cue an even *more* awkward pause.

I suddenly wanted to giggle, but that would be bad. Right?

"It will give you little comfort to know this, but your trial is nearly over. Grey will end the danger," Notte said.

Pinstripe stood. "I don't know who you think you are, but you have no business—"

Notte... *looked* at him.

Do you remember being very small and faced with real authority? It may not have been your parents; could have been a teacher, or a policeman. It may not even have been someone angry. Authority doesn't have to be angry to be terrifying. There is that moment of realizing you are so small, and in so much trouble, and in such danger of shame—discolored with humiliation, stained by all the bad feelings you ever feared were possible, and you would do anything to be acceptable to that authority again.

Just my upbringing, then? All right, then. Happy face.

So anyway, Notte *looked* at him, and the old man stopped as if he'd walked into a wall and the wall had punched him in the stomach.

"I apologize," said Notte, somehow making it worse, as if those words were spoken on the old man's behalf. "You do not know your enemy, and what you do not know will kill you. I must insist you sit down."

Old man sat down. Booyah! (I may have said that out loud. I choose to believe they all looked at me because of my ravishing beauty instead. Glowing, remember.)

"As I have said, your enemy is known as a sliver," Notte continued.

I pointed at Pinstripe and said, "Ha!" (They all stared again, but I choose to believe—well, you know.)

"It is a piece of a magical being who has been torn apart, as I said before," Notte continued, ignoring my outburst. "A piece which has sentience of its own, and constantly hungers for that integrity which it has lost. As a result, it devours whole persons—such as your friends and family—and for a time, mimics them, achieving a sense of wholeness via the victim's echoed memories and personality. Once they have digested what they have taken, the hunger begins again, and the hunt resumes."

"That's so sick," said Cassie, her color gone unappealingly green.

"What difference does this make?" said Pinstripe, red-faced and sweating. His fear tasted like old, bitter orange peels. "What difference does any of this make? We kill them with fire! That is all!!"

I scoffed at him and tilted my chair back again. "It's a sliver. You can't possibly kill them, fire or no."

"I fear Grey is correct," Notte said with far more patience than I deserved. "They cannot be killed in their present form. Those whom you have dispatched will reform and come for you again."

Cassie gasped.

"No. No," camo-Sam said, and started swearing

Both teen boys cursed in colorful street Spanish.

As for me, I leaned all the way back in my chair, hands behind my head, and studied the halogen bulb patterns on the ceiling. Nothing could steal my buzz right now. "It's hopeless for you lot, anyway," I said at normal volume, though nobody was listening. "You don't have the ability to kill them."

And my view was eclipsed by Barry. Barryclipse. Barclipse?

Bald as the moon but a lot more angry, he scowled down at me. "Are you saying none of them are dead?"

"I think that's been said a couple of times now," I tilted my head to the side. "You're blocking my view, Barry."

"Then how do we kill them?"

I tried to see the light patterns behind him by closing one eye, then the other, but no. Barry's moon-head was too big. "Same way we do every night, Pinky: reunite them into one piece and then burn the lot. Do you mind? You're harshing my halogen."

He recoiled as if I'd slapped him. Weird guy.

"Lady and gentlemen, please," said Notte with far greater patience than I could produce. "I do not have much time here. Allow me to instruct you, and then I will be on my way."

"You're not staying?" shrieked Cassie.

"You can't leave us!" cracked the older boy whose name I'd missed. I'm calling him Temporary Jorge, so.

Barry swung back into view. "Where do we need to go to unite the pieces?" he said, his voice rough as if I'd threatened to set *him* on fire.

"Where? Do we need a where?" I looked at Notte upside down, tilting my chair so far back that my hair touched the floor. "Hey, Notte. Do we need to go someplace specific to do this?"

"I would advise it," he said. "Given what will be unleashed the moment you do, you will need the freedom to act without detection. I would advise an empty realm. Perhaps the Plane of Dreams?"

I made such a face. "Oh, that doesn't sound fun at all."

Barry leaned closer. "How do we get to the Plane of Dreams?"

"You already did, big boy, when I kissed you," I said, and waggled my eyebrows.

He didn't react at all this time. No fun.

"One of the realms owned by the Dream should be safe enough for you, yeah," he suddenly said. "How do we get there?"

I scowled. "What do you mean, safe for me?"

"I believe Grey has a portal," said Notte.

Why, he sold me out! The front legs of my chair thocked down like exclamation points. "No. No, I don't. I don't know what you're talking about. I don't have a portal. I don't even have coins that look like portals. No portals here."

"John," said Notte, and his tone took all the rest of my happiness away and squished it into a little ball and then washed it down the food disposal.

"That's supposed to be a secret, you know," I griped as I took it out of my pocket—shiny, silver, the size of an American quarter. "Nobody's supposed to know, but no, everybody knows, and I might as well start charging rent, because—"

"John."

I stopped, clutching my portal tightly, and wouldn't meet his eyes.

Gentler this time. "John. Do you need my help to do this?"

Ouch. No, really, ouch, and not for the reasons you think. He really meant he'd take time off whatever else he was doing to help me, if I asked.

It's funny the way shame sometimes forces you to become a better person. Every time I start to be uncharitable toward him, he does something that reminds me he really does consider me a *friend*—an unfathomable word for Notte—and even though I still don't really understand why he gives me this, it takes away some of my rights to be a little bitch to him.

I mean, I do it anyway, but that's beside the point.

"No. No, I know how to do this." Just because I didn't want to—

"Wait a second, what's going on now?" demanded camo-Sam.

"I am not going to save you," Notte said. "Grey is."

All heads swung to me. Except Barry's, because his was already pointing there.

I cleared my throat. "Well. Now that I know what it is, I can defend myself. I mean slivers are rare, but not unheard of. Yes. Technically. Once the body is altogether, I'll have a couple of minutes to attack it before it reaches full strength. Technically, if nothing goes wrong, I can kill it."

"What?" breathed Temporary Jorge. "How?"

"I'll sing it to death," I said, just to see the looks on their faces. Those looks were worth it, too.

"Music is the method by which he manages magic," said Notte with an absolutely deadpan expression, earning my glare.

Then I had two thoughts in a row. Uncharitable thought: *This would be why Notte let me take so much power from him — so I could take out a creature known to be his enemy.* More mature thought: *No, he'd have given it to me anyway.* Still, it was rather convenient.

"I'm going with you," said Barry.

"No. Nonsense. None of you are going," I said. "You're humans. Are you mad? Do you have any idea how fragile you are? Just the sound-waves from what I have to do would flatten you. You can't come."

They gave me haunted eyes.

I get it. This wasn't coming across as saving-the-day. These were people who'd fought and lost and won and fought some more, and they didn't have any more space in their heads for not fighting. For life after the fight.

I looked at Notte.

He sighed. "I will handle this," said Notte quietly. "However, I believe you should take Mr. Ballas with you."

Wait. Barry's last name was *Ballas*? I coughed to cover my snickering.

"Why him?" demanded Pinstripe.

"It must be done." And Notte's voice changed. His pupils widened, swallowing the green of his eyes, which color seemed suddenly brighter than any eye-color should be.

All the tension went out of my frame. I swayed on my feet, exhaling, and all the others sat down very nicely, as if they'd been asked.

"Go now, my friend," said Notte. "I will take care of these few without harm."

"Are you sure about this?" I said, my own voice dreamy in response to whatever magic he was using. Seriously, I don't know what his magic is. Nobody does. Since they're manufactured, vampires don't technically fall into any of the Seven Peoples' categories.

No, I will not explain that now. This is *my* story, and nobody else's.

"I am certain. Fear not for these few. Go."

How did I go from endearing, wandering minstrel to medieval knight-hero in six short hours? Notte. That's how. I told you he tends to make you more than you are.

Damn his eyes.

I walked out of the dining room, away from these people I'd never see again, unsure how I felt. Was I relieved? Saddened? I didn't know; in a short bit of time, we'd faced death together, learned each other's' names (except for Temporary Jorge), and now, they wouldn't remember any of it.

I shouldn't feel sad. Humans die so quickly anyway. Getting attached is just foolish.

Barry stepped into the elevator foyer with me.

That was a surprise. He didn't look magically relaxed. He looked exactly the same as he had. What was up with that? "What are you doing? Go back," I said.

"No. He's going to mess with their heads. They won't remember any of it, and they'll all wake up in a hospital or something. I don't got time for that, so I'm going with you."

I began to form the notion that Barry had even more experience with the Mythos than I'd surmised. "How did you know what he's going to do?"

"It's standard, isn't it? Since the First War, that's what's been done with humans."

I leaned in and sniffed.

He leaned back, scowling. He smelled human (less offensively than he had before his shower, of course) and he felt human. Sounded human, except for his pesky abnormal word choice.

"Explain yourself," I commanded.

"Not now. We don't got time. Use your portal, Grey." He took a deep, slow breath. "Please."

Please? Well, that carried weight.

I really hate not knowing what's going on. Notte and Barry both knew something, some salient fact to which I was not privy, and yet they expected me to do all the saving here. "Harumph." Yes, I said it out loud. Don't judge.

I studied the coin in my hand; flat, shiny, with the faintest imprint of a throne with tendril-like things growing from its base like mangrove roots. This portal was very old. I wondered if the day would come when its imprint would be completely worn away, even to my eyes. "Not here. We can lure them together in Central Park and go from there."

"People will see," he said, following me into the foyer.

"No, they won't. We can find an isolated spot." I pressed the elevator button and waited for the elevator man to bring the carriage up. Goodness, this place was posh. Barry lived well. "Just so you know, when you're dead, I'm taking all your stuff."

He chortled. "This place isn't mine. My stuff blew up when we took out the bar earlier today. This place is Peterson's."

All Pinstripe's, then. So Barry was homeless? "Oh." And we reached new levels of awkwardness. "Do you have... someplace to stay?"

The elevator arrived before he answered, and that was the end of our 'moment.'

The elevator man smiled and told us to visit Zabar's. Doormen smiled and waved as we left. It all felt... wrong. Eerie. Like an ending, like he wouldn't be coming back—and perhaps he wouldn't. If the old man's memory was altered, he wouldn't know Barry. Would he? "How did you all meet, anyway?" I muttered as we walked past the stained glass hallway.

Barry smiled and waved at the final doormen, and then his smile fell away like a discarded shirt. "I tracked them down," he said, jay-walking.

The middle-aged woman from the bar—no, the sliver who ate her—stood at the cross-street, watching us unblinkingly. My heart-rate sped up. I swallowed hard. I'm not very brave, you know? I didn't like this plan. Yes, it made total sense, and should be possible, but I really didn't like this plan.

The park wasn't far. I had to keep it together. I had to call them to me. But what if some of the slivers were far away? What if four of them converged on me while the others were still miles off? How was I going to do this?

And what had Barry just said? "Tracked them down? How?"

"I could feel them," said Barry. "Marked. You know. Same as you."

Okay, this was disturbing. "You *are* just a human, aren't you?"

He didn't answer me as we entered Central Park, right across from the Museum of Natural History.

Beautiful this time of year. Stark, cold, just beginning to bloom. Loads of people from schoolchildren to the elderly, from single sweaty joggers to nerdy couples holding hands and avoiding scary commitment-causing eye-contact. Whee.

"Come on," said Barry.

The spooky not-a-lady followed us.

I hate tension like this, being chased, slowly like in a nightmare. We walked as if all were well, and I kept my ears magically hidden from casual passersby. I let her follow. I *let* her chase me.

"You need to do more," Barry whispered. "The rest won't come."

You know what? I was too afraid to question his weird acumen anymore. I opened my aura up full-blast.

People slowed as they passed me now, staring at one another in surprise. They didn't even know what they responded to. Sudden peace took them, like a summer concert under the stars with soft blankets and beloved company, like the fireside combination of lonely violin and a partner's not-so-lonely eyes. Soon, people began to smile as I walked by them, and not at me. Nerdy couples joined gazes, not just hands. Old people who'd played chess for a thousand years warmed one another's knobby fingers. Children, too young for romantic love, blossomed in perfect and beautiful friendships on the spot, which would probably last the rest of their lives.

Even Barry looked softer. "Weird how you do that," he muttered.

"It's love," I said, and I don't care how cheesy it sounded. "It wouldn't do us Fey much good if we needed it but couldn't generate it."

"Bees and pollen and flowers, or something," he muttered, and stuck his hands in his pockets. Poor fellow was blushing. Being bald didn't help. I essentially had Rudolph the Red-Skulled Reindeer over here.

A wave of weirdness licked up my back, like an unexpected cold breeze.

I shivered and looked behind, and there she was - still in her evening-out dress and heels, and look at that, she wasn't alone. Three more people stalked with her, all with the same dead hunger. A man in a business suit, a teenage girl in a Catholic school uniform, and a little Chinese boy no older than six marched along in perfect rhythm, parting the foot traffic. They weren't gaining on us, but they weren't falling behind, either.

I turned to face front again, focusing my energy, trying to tempt them in spite of every instinct I had to run and hide because running and hiding would do no good. Their presence here proved that. They really could track me. Blast it all.

"I think I am going to puke," I announced, just as two passing girls giggled and linked their fingers.

"Do it quick, then," said Barry, bastion of warmth and compassion.

Then I noticed something. "Ah, why are you walking in time with the slivers?" Because he was. His step fell in complete rhythm with theirs, *stomp-stomp-stomp-stomp*, and oh, the willies crawled up my spine and widened my eyes and made my ears as stiff as knife-blades. "What are you doing that for?"

"Luring them. Shut up, this takes effort," he said like it was no big, no issue, *not a major deal at all*, and I made a tiny sound I will never repeat for you and you will just have to imagine. "It's almost over," he grunted then, as close to comforting as Barry ever got, and we left the path.

The section of Central Park called the Ramble is wilderness by Manhattan standards. Enterprising humans have used it for sexual liaisons for quite literally a century, and that made it secluded enough for our less-fun purposes. We walked along the water, away from the people, away from the places easy to put feet down, and into the woods.

The isolation was immediate.

Humans really like to follow paths. It's a *thing* for most of them, a way to feel safe and avoid negative repercussion from authority. That worked well for us in this circumstance. Nobody was around.

"Stay concentrated," said Barry, forging over boulders and avoiding tree-roots with almost Fey-like agility.

So he wasn't human. That was obvious. What he was, I had no idea. Anything? Anything. Could be anything. Right. He was on my side, so that mattered. "Notte knows what you are. Why? Did you meet before?"

"Here." He stopped. "I don't have a guitar for you. You just got to sing. Draw them."

"They're not all here yet," I said, looking around. I could feel them coming, feel the strangeness of their hunger—an empty, hollow space, cold and vacuous. I couldn't see them through the trees. Blast it all, where were they?

"Sing, dumbass!" he snarled. "I'll keep them at bay!"

"Sure you will! How? And since when do you use words like, 'at bay'?" I bellowed back.

And the six-year-old boy stepped out of the woods.

I forced aside the stomach-dropping thought that *this had once been a child*, that now he was not, that now he never would again, and somehow made myself sing.

It had never been this hard. The silvers ate light and love and warmth and excreted terrifying cold spots I could feel but not see, and they were coming closer. One by one, clumsy feet crunched twigs and snapped branches, stumbling on hidden roots and loose stones, splashing as one of them walked through the water with zero concern for damp or cold or muck or anything aside from eating me.

Oh, and now they came into view like hobgoblin mannequins, appearing one after another through the leaves and between tree-trunks, all unblinking eyes and no shadows. Then Barry stepped in front of me and held out his arms.

The enemy's advance stopped. One by one, they walked into our little clearing, and then stood there, watching me like the last ice lolly on a hot day.

How was he doing that?

I sang on, afraid because I really no idea what he was, or what he wanted, or what he'd do with me when this was all over. *Never mind never mind never mind*, I told myself, *just sing, sing, sing*, and I sung until my ears vibrated, until the ground under my feet surged with the need for new life, until flowers launched through the soil with time-lapse quickness as if I were Luthien Tinuviel and Barry was really short for Beren.

I knew not what I sang. It boasted fear as its leitmotif, will-power for rhythm, and frigid, wide-eyed adrenaline as its chorale. I sang quick notes, high notes, fast and vicious and stabbing notes, notes that danced like icepicks over a frozen river and threatened to loose all the torrent hidden below.

One by one they came out of the woods, the four I'd seen and two more. I sang. My voice trembled, and my song shook like small birds in a winter storm, but my magic held. My aura—the unique flavor and scent of who I am, of all my *self* and sense and essence—bloomed like the bouquet of oven-fresh bread.

The six stood and watched us, silent and still, unblinking, not a shadow among them. Slivers; probably the source of shadow-eater legend, now that I thought about it, but far scarier because once they all joined, they'd be something worse. They'd be a god, a bad one, a mad one, and I would not have much time to take it down.

There were six of them. This was a good thing. If there'd been seven, they'd make a powerful god, indeed.

"Portal," Barry croaked out.

I felt it in my pocket, smooth and silver, and kept singing as I pulled it out. Every movement slow and graced, I dropped it to the ground.

Rays shot out of it, white and widening on their way to the sky, bars of light that looked solid enough to cut my hands if I grabbed them. "Barry," I sang, and the use of his name in the climbing beauty of my song almost made it funny. "In. Get in. They'll follow me. They'll go through you. They'll follow me to the liiiiiight."

Snicker all you want. It was a moment.

He stepped in, disappearing at once. The moment he did, they advanced. All six of them, steps in time, shadowless and with no clear use for their eyelids. I waited until the last possible second, until I'd have felt their breath if they had any, then jumped in after him.

6 DREAMS

I meant to keep singing through the portal, but the moment I stepped in, everything went wrong.

Portals are supposed to be smooth, yeah? Slick and slippery and sweet to ride, utterly frictionless. Riding a portal made by my people is like flying free, without effort and without weight. Well, not this time. I hit something—some huge, warm, unyielding wall—and hurtled off-course. Out of control, I crashed through the portal's built-in protections like a rock ripping a chain of daisies, flew into the æther, and was lost.

I somersaulted breathlessly through un-space woven from the earth's soul and the wind's blood. I screamed, or tried, but the sound came far away and delayed as if to mock me, as if my voice only played at physics. There was no anchor, no wall, no ground. There was nothing.

Dark things darker than lightlessness flew past, larger than barrels and missing me by inches. I covered my head, uselessly. What were they? Other people trapped here, lost forever? Were they alive? Aiming for me? Was I the one flying at *them*, so they'd think I was attacking?

There was no up and down, no air's friction to slow me, and I wept in utter silence. Eternity ate my form, softening my edges, all my life's sorrow and fear ready to dissipate in one thick and clotted instant.

And then I ripped wetly through something like thin flesh or thick cloth (as if *I* were the solid thing, the thing with weight and reality) and plunged into startling light. Blinded and upside down, I plowed into the ground.

Dead grass and crumbling soil flew as I dug a me-shaped trough, then lay in it, gasping. The fact that that my sob exited my throat like a normal sound just made me sob harder, and I covered my face, alive, present, *real*, and so grateful to be *someplace* that I didn't care what came next.

A strangely dun sky arched overhead, free from detail or cloud. The air slept over brittle grass in utter silence, and hints of cladal magic pooled comatose beneath the dirt. By some miracle, I'd landed in the Plane of Dreams after all.

I was where I was supposed to be, in spite of what had happened—and what had I hit? Things couldn't interrupt portals. That wasn't how portals worked. What happened?

I sat up, stiff as anything, and looked for my portal, but it was gone. It must have broken, truly. One of the few things I kept from my father, gone forever. An uncomfortably guilty weight settled in my chest, followed by fear: how was I going to get home?

A shadow swept over my face, and Barry yanked me to my feet. Scratches and burns replaced his torn-off shirt, and he looked like he'd plowed into the dirt, too. "Can you still sing?" he bellowed, spittle flying and pupils dilated.

I had to sing, didn't I? The slivers were coming, and they'd find us here, regardless of the detour. "Why not?" I answered, my shivering ears bent so far back they nearly hid under my hair.

He nodded. Then he threw me over his shoulder like a proper fireman and took off at a run.

As I already said, why not? This day really couldn't get any weirder.

Bouncing on his back gave me time to reflect on my life. This was all the culmination of my errors, my panicky decisions, my attempts to run away. I shouldn't even have been in New York. I should have been in Chicago, or at least in the Silver Dawning—home sweet home—but noooo, I had to be in Manhattan, proving Merlin wrong, proving my father wrong, proving everybody wrong.

Some tiny part of me wondered, though: if I hadn't gotten involved, who'd would have helped those humans? None of them would have known what to do. Notte certainly wouldn't have come along. Memories altered or no, those people would all be dead if I *hadn't* made my mistakes.

I don't know why that made me feel good. I'm not good. I'm a terrible person, and selfishness is my art form. "What is my life?" I groaned.

Barry didn't answer.

Dead grass flew beneath his heels, only distinguishable from the dirt by a slightly lighter shade of brown. My abs might be impressive, but his shoulder was *slightly* more rigid, and jouncing on it robbed me of breath. Annoyed (and breathless), I braced myself on Barry's sweat-slicked back to look up.

Devoid of obvious light source, the sky stretched over us like a dull blanket, ordinary Plane of Dreams fare. Absolutely nothing interrupted the flatness of this place—earth as smooth as if it had been steamrolled, no hills, and no real horizon-line because the sky and earth matched colors where they met.

But wait. Trees shaded the horizon like a wall of vague broccoli, conspicuous in a slightly darker shade of dun, and *that* was not standard Plane of Dreams fare at all. They were too far off to determine anything other than their essential tree-ness, but they still shouldn't have been here. The Plane of Dreams was empty; all its denizens slept hidden between dimensional walls, where nobody could ever touch them again. There were no things to interact *with*, not even regular light, and there certainly weren't trees. So where the hell had we landed?

Then the slivers came, and I stopped caring about anything else.

They landed like meteors, foreign and destructive, erupting grass and dirt with the force and etheric power of their crashes. They shook the earth, making Barry stumble. And then it got worse.

There were no binding powers here, no shielding or careful wards, and the slivers' stolen human forms immediately broke. Half-hidden in the craters they'd made, they quivered, distorted, and their limbs expanded to knobby trunks or shrunk to flailing tendrils. For no reason, their heads expanded like balloons, and the little boy's eyes *stretched until they tore* and distributed across his whole mis-shapen cranium.

That's when I stopped watching. Good thing I hadn't eaten lunch.

The slivers were returning to blob things like the one that attacked us in Barry's bar, and hey, I could run so much faster than my human counterpart that I no longer appreciated the ride. "Put me down! Put me down!"

Instead, Barry jumped.

When I say "jumped...."

Ever thought what it all must look like from a grasshopper's perspective? More specifically, from the grasshopper's back-end? How the world falls away like it tripped over a cliff, and the ground's details go so small? One weightless moment at the peak flipped my stomach as we began our descent.

Dark, crooked limbs sliced into the earth *where we'd just been*, stabbing into the sleeping ground and creaking like old doors.

I might have screamed.

My stammering brain managed to put it all together. Trees. Living, moving trees, guardians of the sleeping members of the Dream. Which could only mean we were not in the ordinary Plane of Dreams, where anyone could go, but we'd somehow penetrated into the actual between-realm where the Dreams lived.

I wanted to deny it. Nobody could get in here. This was where the People of the Dream slept, creatures almost no one had seen in thousands of years apart from the random escaped sylph or naiad. This was impossible. This was im-freaking-possible.

We came down on the other side, and Barry landed wrong, stumbled forward, and hurled me off his back harder than I liked. We'd lucked out: the guard-trees stopped chasing us and instead went for the slivers, drawn by their destructive and flaring power. They slid through the dirt like boats through waves, roots hidden deep, and in spite of myself, I stared after them.

"They won't ignore us forever," said Barry.

Of course they wouldn't. We were foreign contaminants. "My portal's gone." My voice broke. Tears—stupid, inconvenient, embarrassing tears—stole my vision and glossed everything like Vaseline on a lens. My portal. The one thing I'd kept from my family—

I must have been lost in this thought for a moment too long. "Hey!" Barry yelled, and slapped me.

"Dick!" I yelled, and slapped him back. We breathed angrily at one another for a moment.

"We gotta move," said Barry with an unspoken *you're the dick*, which I wasn't, but whatever. I got up stiffly and we took off at a jog.

The problem remained. This wasn't a place with left-over exits or other travelers who might give us a lift. We couldn't *defend* against trees, either. I mean you know what roots can do to solid stone in time. Have you ever seen trees take down an entire fortress? I have, and these guard-trees would not need the benefit of years.

Creaking branches and the sharp sound of splintering made me look back. The slivers were winning, sort of—destroying trees, smashing wood, and consequently summoning more battalions of broccoli-shapes from the distance. If the slivers were any ordinary monsters, numbers would win out in the end, but they were not ordinary. Soon they'd join and become a god, and then we were all in trouble. The trees had no way to know that. They were *trees*. "Lovely day for a walk, yeah?" I said as we ran, trying to lighten the situation.

"They're pissed," Barry said.

"How would you know? Maybe this is an ordinary day for them." A wall of tree-shapes approached from the left, so we ran away from them and into open and disorienting emptiness. Dead grass crunched under my feet, but the sound came thick, muffled, like this whole place had its fingers in its ears.

"Because *I'm* pissed," said Barry, and stumbled again.

I pulled him up so we could keep jogging. His arm felt human. His weight felt human, and his temperature. No weird power wafted off him, and he'd ceased to jump like an overgrown bald grasshopper. "Right, then, oh piss-ed one," I said, adding syllables just because. "What are you?"

Another crack of broken wood pattered the grass behind us with splinters. Only a big, powerful hit could take these trees out, and the slivers even hadn't merged yet. I'd grossly under-calculated. We were in so much trouble.

"You wouldn't like the answer," Barry said, breathing too hard, face too red, his sweat too sudden and too cold.

"Don't tell me I have to carry *you* now. Ew," I said, though I was more than ready to do it. We were united here, whatever he was, and... well. He'd saved my life. At least right now, he wasn't my enemy.

"No. That'd be stupid." He shoved me off, then stumbled again.

"At this rate, they'll catch us before we can get to a safe enough distance to sing." I hoisted him up again and pulled his arm around my neck.

"Dumbass," he mumbled, but let me. Now, we moved at *my* speed.

We're fast, we Fey of the silver tongues and leaf-shaped ears. Fast enough to avoid being seen, fast enough to escape hunters of Darkness and other predators, fast enough to outrun anything that thinks we make sweet and tasty snacks. Carrying him was easy (apart from the sweat, which *was* gross). Barry had saved me, so I would save Barry. Simple.

And besides, my curiosity was burning me up. "So among the Mythos, who are you?" I said, tugging him more tightly over my shoulders. "Seriously, now. You're obviously not Fey. You're not of the Sun, and definitely not Darkness. Some kind of Kin, maybe? Or, ooh, perhaps you're of the Dream! That would make a lot of sense, with all that's happening here."

He didn't answer, and behind us, the sound of ruined wood ceased. The next battalion of tree-guards was too far off. There was nothing between us and the slivers now but space. Great!

"I can keep babbling, or you can answer my query," I said. "Obviously, you're something with pied-piper powers, the way you were able to lure those things with your footsteps. Not that those powers work on me, of course. You *do* know I kissed you just to be annoying?"

He grunted.

"Maybe you're a dryad's son, or something," I said. "Or maybe even a crazy three-way mix, with Fey and Dream and human all rattling around in your veins like mismatched screws in a toolbox, and none of it lines up, and so maybe some days parts of you are Fey or parts of you are Dream or—"

"Stop." He jerked as if to pull away from me, and was slippery enough with sweat that he nearly succeeded.

I pointed at him. "You're part kitsune."

He stared as if seeing me for the first time. "The hell I am."

"Because they jump really high." I beamed at him. "Made you look."

"Just sing, you nutty bastard."

There he went with out-of-character speech again. I lay him down on the grass, knowing it pricked him, but there was nothing for it. "Stay down. I'll aim high; the magic should pass over you so you might survive this."

He nodded.

Time to sing.

I closed my eyes and pushed it all away: away with the fear, away with the tension, away with the dead trees and approaching, hungry doom, until nothing remained but me and the song I would weave. I crouched until my downturned hands hovered inches above the earth, and the earth resonated back to me. A tickling hum kissed my palms and vibrated my teeth, and if my hair had been short, it would have stood on end. Instead, my ears pointed out and up, quivering like thin leaves in front of a subwoofer. My eyes glowed. Lights like fairie-glimmers appeared under my skin, floating as if I were a galaxy and they my wandering stars. To me, all this dull, dumb world grew brighter, cleaner, alive and awake and aware.

I wove my hands in a graceful pattern, finding and shaping the sound-waves invisible to those not of Fey blood, and the stiff, dead grass quivered with my growing power. My voice reached for timbres and tones it had not done since I'd left home, and the wordless song stretched me, tested my poorly-used skills. But training held; I found my rich baritone and unearthed my sweet tenor, my entire range clear as spring melt.

The words formed in me and I sang them, following their call, obeying their own need for wholeness even as I called *something else* to be whole.

"Be whole, be whole, remember no more the breaths between thee and thy skin of before.

"Be whole, be whole, remember thy frame as the heart calls its blood and the blood beats its claim.

"Be whole, be whole, remember no more the deep blade that carved thee and shattered thy core."

Silvertongue doesn't translate well into English. Use your imagination. It was *good*.

I sang it again and stood, raising my hands to face the dull sky, sending out the sounds like weird aural missionaries. I sang, and my lungs ached, and my throat warned it would pay me back later, but for now, *for now*, it did what I asked.

And just like I'd warned the warned pinstripe, it happened: *my power came forth*.

It spread from my feet like a pool of melted silver, heating the air, bending and snapping dead grass with raw will. Contracting and obeying all around me for miles in diameter, the whole world *throbbed*—one deep and breath-stealing beat so penetrative it blinded. I timed it with my heart, each thump slow enough to invoke the feel of bodies in tandem, and I threw my head back and *sang*.

The slivers came, slow but focused, still twitching and trembling like pustules about to burst. I sang, and I willed them together. To remember. To know each other, and as they came toward me, to converge.

They glorped into one another like drunken fiends, their pace toward their partners quickening as though they were made of ferrous and magnetized metals.

Half a mile away: they bumped together, absorbing, joining, somehow gaining no more size but much more solidity. They merged like drops of mercury, seamlessly losing demarcating lines and details.

A quarter mile away: only three remained, and they would become two before twenty more feet passed beneath them.

I altered my tune, weaving subtle and complex song-craft only the finest master-singer could construct. I knitted in mines and magical knives. I wove nooses made of notes pulled just tight enough to dent the song's skin. I tied garrotes ready to pull and behead the beast that emerged. I sang and I trembled, true royal power flooding my veins and setting my skin alight. And then, in one brief second of weakness, I glanced Barry's way.

Instead of lying down, he stood, leaning away from me as if I were a wind machine and he was trying to avoid being sucked closer and chopped to pieces.

Teeth bared, hands curved into taut and trembling claws, all his color gone... he shouldn't react like that. My power ought to be flattening him, pushing him away, not pulling him closer. My voice caught, tripping over bad concentration.

"Keep... doing it!" he strained, and gasped, and leaned closer for one moment before pulling away.

My song faltered completely and I stopped, though the song didn't fade right away—I'd filled the air with too much, and it lingered, effective for a time. The slivers, still forming into some unreasonable shape, blorbled and hissed at a distance, but I couldn't take my eyes from Barry Ballas. Barry, whose once-familiar form warped and skewed in the fading notes of my song.

"Barry?" I whispered.

"Don't got a lot of time." He labored over every word, eyes fixed on me—no, *gaze* fixed on me, because one eyeball sort of rotated to look inside his skull instead.

"Barry?" The whisper surprised me. I couldn't speak louder—and not because my voice was tired.

"To the trees. Sing. Bring them... me. Bring. The trees will help you."

They'd attack me, too, wouldn't they? "Barry!"

He faltered. Looked up. And pinned, nailed all of his strength and energy and will in the heart of one crucial word: "Run!"

I took a step back, obeying without thinking.

His feet left the earth. He didn't change, he didn't visibly alter, but he *rose* like flames with gasoline thrown on them. Fiery sun-like power as hot and deadly as fusion darkened his skin. "Run!"

I ran. I ran, sickened, too panicked to stay and argue, too weak to stay and disobey that *presence.* A fresh wall of tree-guardians approached, knee-deep in the kindling of their fallen brethren and bolstered by rows of trees on the march from the distance. Tall dark wood and stabby limbs with translucent leaves, they came, sluicing through the soil in eerie, wrong silence and leaving furrows in their wake. I ran toward them, completely unsure what would happen, not daring to look back lest watching Barry change would change my course.

Barry. A sliver? Couldn't be. He'd helped me. Wanted me to destroy the other slivers. What the hell was going on?

The trees were distracted by three crazy power sources, and I ducked between their thick, rough boles, dodging swinging sharp branches and protruding roots. The trees ignored me; the greater threat came in my wake, drawn by the sound of my song which lingered like perfume. I stopped in a temporary clearing, surrounded by the trees' splintered dead, and gasped.

Barry still hovered where I left him, but he didn't look the same. His usual hard, humorless expression was gone, replaced by something hungry and wild with raze-it-to-the-ground joy. He held his hands out, waiting for the remaining two dark blobs to reach him.

They did. And they joined.

They slid into his hands and up his fingers, staining his veins until they stood out under his pale skin like tributaries of Acheron. They melted into him and as they did, he grew, not in stature, but in *presence,* in strength, in *self,* merging, becoming one.

Because, damn it all with everything I've ever used to curse, there weren't six slivers. There were seven. The seventh was Barry, and this mad, bad god was once again whole.

He laughed then, a sound I felt in shockwaves that slammed into and through me like blooming rings of fire, robbing me of vitality even from this distance. I doubled over, gut-punched and gasping burning air. It was time to act, *right now*, before he reached full power.

Barry had given me enough time.

I gathered the strings and threads of my song between my fingers like spiderwebs, pulling from the circle of ethereality around me and the trees and Barry the broken god. I hummed, spinning sound-threads with slow and careful grace into a vibrating sphere that held itself, invisible and trembling, against my palms. My heartbeat pulsed through it, causing brief flickers of light in its unseen depths, and I shuddered, my skin suddenly too sensitive against the brush of my clothes, the air, everything.

I took a deep breath. I closed my eyes. *I'm sorry, Barry,* I thought, and then I sang.

He hadn't reached full strength, not quite yet, and for some insane reason he he'd either forgotten me or chosen to ignore what I was doing. My sound and the power in my hands passed harmlessly between the trees and expanded, grew, flattening grass and thrusting dirt up in ripples the shape of sound waves.

When it hit him, a sound like the clash of every cymbal in the world rent the air in two.

It distorted the light, twisted the sound of my voice and came at me like fire-filled backdraft. I braced myself almost too late, feet digging into the dirt, my arms forward and my hair streaming behind me. Heat, *such heat*, embraced and kissed and tried to kill me, for this was a god, this was a member of the People of the Sun, and he oozed strength and the cleansing destruction of fire.

Somehow, I stood my ground, sucked in air so hot it burned my lungs, and sang.

Red glowing lines like cracks in a kiln appeared all over his body, and he roared. His feet hit the ground, so heavy he shook leaves from their branches. Fractured, he wavered for one moment, then ran at me.

Every step he took sent me nearly off my feet. Every inch he neared burned more, and hurt, and then the trees in the very front wave of the wood army burst into flame.

No, no, no, Barry had given me this, arranged this, maybe sacrificed himself for this, and I *would not run.* Faces flashed before my eyes—my father, my grandmother, Katie, Merlin, Notte, insane people who believed in me when I thought I knew better—and *I sang back,* not as loud as his roar but every bit as powerful.

The cracks in him grew wider, fracturing, and he stumbled, robbed of coordination. He struggled for integrity. To find his wholeness again, fully, completely, so he could devour me.

Maybe Barry had betrayed me. Maybe Barry had saved me. I refused to see the first one for now, and I sang. His will pushed against mine, so much bigger, but not whole. I had the advantage. *Die,* I thought, and I sang. *Die! DIE!*

His left leg cracked and blew off in a vomit of orange fire, and he fell to the earth. "Elf!" he roared, and I suddenly knew that when Barry had said that word before it had been teasing and fond and not at all like this, not with *hate* and *hunger* and *loathing,* and still he came, clawing up enormous clots of earth with his hands.

I held my ground, bringing my hands together to shape my sound into a funnel. He was close enough now, and I gave him both barrels.

Jagged pieces the size of my fist broke off him and tumbled away, caught in the wind-like power of my song. He reached the first line of trees, and the mere touch of his flailing, dirt-covered arms lit them with a fire so hot they crumbled to ash in seconds, and *still he came.*

I sang.

Pieces the size of melons flew off him now, tumbling away and leaving his face and body living renditions of cubism, and still he came. The second row of trees lit on fire, more slowly, but just as fatal. Without voices to scream, they swayed in pain, creaking and groaning as they died.

Still, he came.

And I sang.

Twenty feet. One arm left now, half a head, his eye fixed on me with terrifying intelligence and determination that we would both die today.

I stood my ground, and I sang.

He slowed. Pieces orange-edged with cinders broke away from him and tumbled to rest at the foot of singed trees, which smothered them in dirt. He crawled, he inched, and finally, he could move no more.

He kept his eye on me the whole time I sang, digging into my mind, making sure I knew I was murdering him. No insanity burned here; hatred, pure and insatiable, he delivered to me at the end of his everything. His eye was the last to go, a glaring, too-aware remnant in a pile of ash.

I sang.

His light winked out, and the last of him drifted away in fading embers that flickered and faded to grey.

Silence.

I fell onto my ass. Panting, hands shaking, so exhausted and so weak I didn't think I could ever get up again. Even if the damn trees decided to mulch me, I couldn't move again. Could not.

Barry. I didn't... what happened here?

Trees came closer, like triffids. I didn't care. It was over. *Barry... I'm sorry, Barry.*

Two trees sluiced in front of me, halting in the dirt like expert skiers, and their branches came together in a skein that hurt my eyes to look at. It was filled with runes I didn't know and couldn't comprehend, intricate with meaning that went beyond my poor taxed brain. Then, the trees ripped the skein apart.

Instead of broken twigs, they parted the air like a curtain.

I stared like an idiot, completely incapable of translating this into anything meaningful for me.

The trees waited with the patience of... trees.

It was some kind of portal. A hole in the air, which they obviously wanted me to go through. None of the trees reached to help me, maybe because they weren't really supposed to be helping me at all. They were antibodies, and I was a germ—and instead of killing me, they were giving me a way out?

That thing could go anywhere. It could be a portal to hell.

Then a strident taxi-horn wafted through, a brash and blatant and beautiful sound. I hadn't used all my adrenaline, apparently, because I was able to rock back and forth until I could roll forward onto my knees and then stand.

The hole was above my head, and I'd have to jump to it. I had no music left in me to help. Blackness licked at the edges of my vision, threatening the end of wakefulness, but I had to try.

My stupid little hop shouldn't have worked, but the hole exuded some kind of vacuum effect, and it sucked me up and through, out of the Plane of Dreams, away from what was nearly my greenhouse-tomb.

I no longer cared where it took me. I fell, and as my vision failed completely, a brief impression of high-rises going the wrong way told me I was upside down, hurtling toward ground familiar with shops and people and fire hydrants, and then

With the worst music hangover I'd ever had in my life, I woke up.

This was a canopy bed, an honest-to-Mab canopy bed, and I lay propped upright by a thousand pillows.

Every single inch of me hurt as if I'd been trampled by horses. Even my ears ached—and Fey ears are extremely fine and sensitive membrane, thank you very much, so that was worrisome. I reached up to make sure they were still whole, still fine as washed silk against my fingertips, and only after that was done considered that I had no blooming clue where I was.

Luxurious came to mind, though in an utterly unrealistic way, like someone had taken an old painting of a glorified imagining of nobleman's lives and made it real. Rich cloth in deep jewel tones draped the walls in artful arches and cordoned off my four-poster bed. The wallpaper glittered with gold patterns in the soft candle-light, and dark wood furniture crouched in the shadows, carved with more decorative flourishes than my first dress-uniform. And I wasn't alone.

He sat in the dark, his eyes completely in shadow. His posture was perfect, and he the picture of gentility and calm. And yet.

And yet.

Seeing him, feeling him the way those among the Mythos feel, I recoiled. The predator was *there*, tightly held, under control but never calm. His possessiveness stifled me like grave clothes. The dark stillness of him shot tension into my nerves as if he readied to pounce, and I knew: if I were a human, he'd have had me. He'd have taken me already.

But I'm not human. I'm nothing he can transform into his vast and monstrous family. I have nothing to fear from Notte. But in that moment, I knew what he was.

He was hunger. He was night.

I closed my eyes, my heart pounding in my ears, and told myself to calm the hell down. Whatever else he was, Notte was my friend.

Then he leaned forward into the gentle candle-light and transformed into a sculptor's dream, a man whose pretty face inspires poetry and whose unnaturally green eyes inspire trust. They filled with concern as he studied me. "John?"

My tension evaporated. "Hi." The moment of terror was past. He'd take care of me. I wanted to whine at him; I hurt, everything was nasty, it was all miserable and everything had gone wrong, and Barry. Barry.

My eyes filled.

"I am so sorry, my friend," Notte said gently, and handed me a fine silk handkerchief as blue as his suit.

I took it. "Sorry?" And I said the first thing that came into my head. "Please don't tell me you knew he was a thing."

"Yes," he said softly. "I knew he was 'a thing.' So did he—but there was no other way to end this."

I closed my eyes, rocked, overwhelmed and under-equipped. "Please explain this to me."

He leaned back and poured a cup of fragrant tea from the small barley-twist side table. "Slivers are terrible things. They devour all they touch, and once sated, steal the form of those whom they have victimized. You know this."

The shadowless woman peering up at my window.... "Yes."

He handed me the tea, and let me warm my hands and inhale the steam before speaking again. "There are times when those whom the slivers devour are stronger—in terms of willpower, stronger—than the slivers themselves."

I looked at him.

"The man known as Barry Ballas was... remarkable," said Notte softly, and I knew in that moment that he regretted Barry's loss more than I did. He loves humans; he even admires them, mad as *that* is. "When eaten, when devoured, his essential self—his will, his thoughts, his mind—overwhelmed the sliver that took him, at least for a time. He had only a small amount of that time; the process of absorption would eventually end him, but while he had control, he used it well."

I put my head back against the pillow and closed my eyes, clutching the teacup like a fine porcelain anchor. "I don't believe you. He was alive. That was a real man. I even managed to piss him off."

"Yes, he was alive, in the same way one who suffers from cancer lives. He lived, being eaten. He chose. He remained in control, and he made his decisions based on what had to be done."

"So he was a hero? Is that it?" I grimaced and rubbed my face; even my cheekbones hurt. "A hero in a bartender's smock."

"He was."

"And you knew?" I looked at him.

"Before you accuse me, my friend, would you have had the courage to do what had to be done had you known?"

I knew he'd ask that. Damn his eyes. "No."

"Hate me if you wish." He sounded truly sorry, and I knew he was. Hard choices were his forte, though he never hardened because of them. "Barry Ballas knew he could never regain his own self. He wished to stop these creatures. What he did was his choice, my friend, entirely his. I aided him out of respect for his decision."

"How did you know all this? I didn't see you two talk. Did the wind tell you, or something?"

He smiled, a secretive, and terrifying thing.

What could I say to this besides a stream of swear words? "Why did he bring me along to play hero? Couldn't someone else have—" Lost him. "—done this?"

"The bait had to be one marked by the creature, and only you, of all those marked, had the ability to fight back."

I wanted to go on thinking of Barry as if nothing had changed. As if he'd had his memory wiped like the rest, and was getting back to life. Claiming insurance for his bar. Making plans for next Christmas. I didn't want this. I didn't like it. "We still could have used any of them for bait, and maybe sent another among the Mythos far more powerful than I. Someone who could've protected the stupid Ever-Dying human and still got the job done."

"You and I both know no human would have returned alive from the Plane of Dreams."

I really didn't like that because he was right. "Especially not where we ended up. Barry made sure we went to occupied territory, you know." He'd hijacked the god's powers to do it. Of course. That was what happened to my portal. *You owe me a portal, dumbass,* I thought, and almost started to cry.

"I believe Barry wished to take no chances with your survival. Therefore, help was required—help that would demand no explanation or repayment."

Automated guard-trees. That fit the bill.

I lay silent for a while. "So who was he? Before."

"Barry Ballas, Manhattan bartender."

I glared. "I know that much. I meant before he was eaten."

"I fear I know less than you do, as you have spent more time with him. May I ask why?"

Because I wanted to make sure his family was taken care of. I wanted other people to know they'd had a hero in their midst. I wanted... I wanted him to not be dead. Grim and humorless and all of that, he still shouldn't be dead.

This was ridiculous. I'd end up writing a ballad if I kept this up. "Because. Loose ends, and all."

"I suspect," Notte said slowly, "that he took care of his affairs before throwing his remaining reserves into this. I doubt there are loose ends for you to find."

That didn't make me feel much better.

"Are you all right, my friend?" Notte said.

"No. But I... I have to be." Silence stretched between us like tar, ripping under its own weight.

Notte put his hand on mine. "Rest. Recover. Do not feel the need to leave until you are ready. I will care for you until that time, however long it takes. I will also provide you with travel aid when you are ready to go home." With that, he rose and left, closing the door softly behind him.

I sighed, exhaling grief, leaking weariness.

I was wrong, for the record. This wasn't my story at all. It was Barry's. The story of a simple human so strong and so steady that he was able to overwhelm the god that ate him, at least for a little while. A soul I never really knew... and now I never will.

Maybe I should write that ballad, after all.

From the Author

Thanks so much for reading! I really hoped you enjoyed this glimpse into the world of Among the Mythos, a science-fantasy series covering 15,000 years.

Visit **AmongTheMythos.com** for the Wiki (always in progress), message boards, and more.

Also, you may want to join the mailing list. I tend to give books away.

I hope you'll be kind enough to leave me a review! Thanks again for taking the time to read.

Read on for a special
preview of *The Sundered.*

1 FLOODED

The world I know is flooded.

The water's black. You don't go in the water. You don't touch it. If you do, it will get you, drag you down, and you're gone. You're only safe from the black water in boats or on land, at least if you're a human. The Sundered can do anything they want in the water. Who knows why?

I believe the world wasn't always this way—that once there was land that stretched forever and water that held no danger—but that doesn't set me apart. What sets me apart, makes me different, is I believe it can go back to that.

"Hey, Harry!" Toddy, one of my younger Travelers, points at something. He straddles the black water, each boot on a different tuft, standing with the easy balance we all must learn or else we die. "There's something over there!"

I hate the tufts—knobs of land sticking out of the water, covered with limp grass like dirty hair. If there are a lot of them, we have to carry the boats. "Coming! Hold on!" Balancing my skiff on my back, I hop toward him, nodding at my Travelers who move to other tufts so there's room for me to leap past.

I don't really give a damn what Toddy wants. Whatever he has to show me, it's not the Hope, the reason I'm out here in this screwed-up place. But I'm young. I can fake interest.

The last space between us is water. I put the skiff in, untie the paddles, and skim toward him.

"There are eyes," Tod says, crouching now as I float near. "Over there, in the water. It's a Sundered One, I'm sure of it."

Sundered? Here? "That's weird. We're not near any cities or catching grounds."

"Think he's unclaimed? He must be!" Tod whispers excitedly. "Can I claim him? If he's unattached, I mean? Can I?"

"No." Damn, I said it too sharply—there's hurt in his eyes. "No," I say again, more gently. "We don't know what tier he is. What if he pulls a reversal on you?" I give myself points for not mentioning he flunked out of Sundered training.

Toddy nods, trying to be grown-up about this, but I've hurt him.

Later. I'll fix it later. Now, I skim where he pointed.

I see more tufts. I see black water, still and dark as far as the horizon in all directions, swallowing my world. I see—there it is. Round eyes bulge out of water, over a hint of skin that looks freakishly orange.

This thing isn't even close to high-tier. I just feel it, the way I'd know what kind of pie it was by putting it in my mouth. The Sundered One realizes I'm staring at it seconds too late, and ducks under as if it thinks it can hide.

Why is it out here? Sundered only run wild in the southern tip of the world. I can feel it's unclaimed—that slick-slime mind, ugly and incomplete, parts of its psyche frozen and alive but not really functional, not really *there*. It's so low-tier there's no point categorizing it. Toddy might be able to handle it, but I already said no, and to go back on my word is to regress as a leader.

It's free and unclaimed, and Sundered are worth money, so that means it's mine.

I half-close my eyes, focus my will, and tighten my grip around that worn mind.

It reacts to me and tries to run away, but this one has been claimed before. It—his—mental spaces almost fit me, edges dulled, and it's no effort at all to hold him tight. Into that mind, into those ruined Sundered thoughts, I plunge—and then I pull.

Pull with will and thought and purpose, like lifting a weakly struggling thing out of thick, sucking mud. The mind suddenly comes free as easily as lifting my own head, and I know he's mine.

That was too easy. He won't be worth much. "Come up and let me see you."

He hears the words. Sundered have different ears than we do. Any vibrations seem to get through. He obeys and clambers onto the tufts.

He looks like a frog. An orange frog-man, with bumps all over, with a wide, flat mouth and big googly eyes too far apart for a man's but not wide enough for an animal's. His spine curves so much he almost seems meant to go on all fours.

Really low-tier.

Toddy gasps, my Travelers paddle closer to see, but I don't look at them right now. I'm fitting my brain to this little guy's. "Ugly, aren't you?"

He sort of ducks twice, acknowledging what I said with a humility so low it's self-hate, and I realize he's got suction-cups on each fingertip and webs between his fingers. Wow. *Really* low-tier, then.

"What's your name, Sundered One?"

"Gorish," he says.

Toddy tells the others how he spotted this one, so it's sort of his even though it's not. I want to find that endearing. I want to. I can't. I've been out here too long. "Hello, Gorish. You know you're mine now, right?"

"Oh, yes, master," he says, doing that ducking thing again and again and again.

An unclaimed Sundered in the middle of nowhere. This is really weird.

My mind goes in all the usual directions. Why is he here? Could this have something to do with the Hope? Am I missing some important clue because I'm messing around with him instead of watching?

Maybe there's no Hope involved, and he just pulled a reversal on his former owner and got away.

Yeah, right. Not this little guy. He couldn't fight his way out of a wash bucket. Maybe his owner died. That would explain his condition.

I can't question him now, anyway. If I do it wrong, if I sound stupid in the eyes of my Travelers, I could lose them. "I need a place to make landfall, Gorish. You know anywhere around here like that?"

"Oooh, yes, master!" the orange guy says, and he starts to caper. He dives in and out of the water, back up onto the tufts, showing off, or—no, he's just playing because it's something he knows how to do.

This guy's head is *shattered.* Whoever claimed him last was rougher on his mind than I am. "Lead the way, Gorish. It's getting dark, and we have to set up camp by then."

So Gorish does.

I say nothing as we paddle, my single-person skiff cutting through the black water. This wasn't the direction I was going. Gorish is leading us completely away from the tufts, further west than I'd planned.

I see some land, tiny islands, nothing but bald mounds of mud. What we need is a simple matter of size: what can handle eight people and all their gear, their tents, and a fire, but has a slope gentle enough that nobody rolls into the water in the middle of the night and vanishes forever?

Like all Sundered Ones, Gorish just knows where proper landfall is.

This one is almost flat, a mass of mess rising from the water. I whirl my hook-and-rope over my head and send it hard into the mud, anchoring myself so I can pull my boat to shore. My boots make sucking noses. This is one messy landfall.

Nobody cares.

Messy is worth solid land, worth the relief of space between us and the water. Tents and voices rise, and our boats line the shore like silent guardians.

We'll rest well tonight. We're going to need it.

I'm more tired than I thought, but I shouldn't be surprised. Claiming a Sundered One is never easy, even one as broken as this. "Demos."

My right-hand man stops and looks at me, his shaved head glinting with the barest hint of blond stubble. "Yeah?"

"Get the buckets to Gorish. He'll fetch the water."

Demos nods, pleased with me. I sit a little straighter. If Demos approves, it was a good decision.

Gorish bounds around camp, splashing like crazy in the shallows and scooping up water in the buckets we give him. He can do that safely. We can't.

Black water is dangerous when it's part of the sea that covers our world, but separate it—in a bowl, a cup, a bucket—and suddenly it's just water, safe to drink, safe to cook with, safe for bathing. Nobody knows why.

Will the Hope have the answer? I was taught it does. I want to believe it does. The alternative is ignorance and extinction. Doom.

Kaia, one of only two females in my group, whoops suddenly, and when I look over, I see her biting into an apple, crunching through the skin.

What? What? Whose idea was this? "Hey!"

Everybody freezes, guilty, but not guilty enough. Tomas has his hand in the apple bag, and he has the gall to grin at me.

"What the hell are you doing?" I demand.

"Hey, Harry," says Tomas, drawing the words out as if to give himself more time to come up with a crap excuse. "You want an apple?" He holds out the bag, challenging me, daring me to argue.

This is one of those tests again.

I've led these people for two years. I shouldn't be tested anymore. Yes, I got the post from my father, but I can do this, and I've proven it, dammit all. "Tomas. Put them back."

He takes another bite, watching me lazily.

Hard to believe this ass is Demos' younger brother. "Put it back. That one you're eating gets detracted from your next meal. You've cost Kaia her next apple, too." I close the distance between us and take back the bag.

We have limited resources. We travel for weeks sometimes without seeing another human being. This was nothing more than stupid arrogance.

Tomas shrugs and turns away, like none of it matters at all.

My heart beats too hard. What did he think I was going to do, let him have the bag?

Maybe he did think that. Demos lets him get away with anything.

"You okay, Harry?" says Sandra quietly.

"Yeah, I'm okay." I tie the bag again. Hopefully, the Sundered power that keeps these apples from going bad wasn't borked by this.

Kaia rolls her eyes and licks her lips at me, like she thinks she's being sexy. Um, no.

Sandra smiles. "Good. Don't let him get to you. He's a dumb-ass."

I'm surprised into laughing. She walks off to do something with her tent.

I calm down. I haven't lost them. My Travelers are still here.

I need them. They're my backbone, my help. Father taught me this. But Tomas pushes the limits sometimes.

I tie the bag up and put it back, and after a few minutes, things go back to normal. Demos and Jax place small stakes tied with string in a circle around our tiny camp, making a minimal barrier— just something to remind us not to wander too far at night.

I feel so weary now. "Hey. Gorish."

My new little orange guy comes bouncing up to me, crouching over like a misshapen frog. "Yes, master!"

"Are there any other people close by?"

"Oh, yes, master!" He holds his hands out wide and spins in a circle, encompassing the world.

I forgot I'm talking to an idiot. "Close by human standards?"

"Oooh." His eyes go all big. "No, master. Not for days that way, or that way, or that way, or that way."

North, South, East, West. Oh, yeah, this one's a winner. Maybe he's so dumb his old master just let him go. Low-tier don't live all that long, anyway. If I over-use him, there'll be nothing left to sell. "All right. Relax. Take it easy. We won't need you for a while."

He stares at me, mouth hanging open. Okay. Don't know what I said that was so shocking.

"Harry." Demos walks up, carrying a pot filled with ingredients for tonight's dinner.

Boiled things. Bleh. "Yeah, good choices. Wait—take out a few of the carrots. According to the Sundered One, we're a long way from any city. I don't want to run out."

"Ooh, carrots," says Gorish.

I look at him. I swear he's pleading like a puppy.

Eh, why not? "Demos? Give me a carrot."

Demos hands me one without arguing. He's the reason I haven't kicked Tomas out. If I do, I might lose him. If I do, I might lose them all.

The carrot makes Gorish so happy he trills like a bird.

Enjoy it now, Sundered. Tomorrow won't be an easy day.

My map is the most priceless thing I own.

My father, grandfather, his father and his father before him all wrote on it, marked it. It lists known cities, predator-rife areas, places with tufts too numerous to paddle through. There's no mark for how many weeks it takes to go from one city to another, but you learn that as you go. This map is the real inheritance of an Iskinder. There's no other like it, anywhere in the world.

By my calculation, we have eight days of full food portions, and we're eight days from any city I know of, if we're careful.

Easy. Easy. Deep breath. We'll be all right.

Old, familiar fear settles in my belly, keeping me quiet. I fear that rushing to find civilization means I'll miss the Hope, fear that the immediate need for survival will eclipse the long-term, and I'll fail.

I won't miss it. I can't. Calm down, Harry.

Dinner is done and the sun sets. The guys laugh, crouching nude around their bucket on one side of the fire, washing the sweat and travel-nastiness from their bodies. The ladies crouch on the other side, separated only by the flames.

Sometime in the past, we used to have showers and baths. We used to be able to swim—a terrifying concept. We used to be able to hook up plumbing with ease, on our own, without high-tier Sundered help. That was before the water turned bad.

These days, most cities can't afford it. We're used to bathing semi-publicly, using buckets.

I have to believe it can go back to the way it was, or I'm wasting my life. Or there's no hope for anyone at all.

I can't sleep. Out here, that matters. Sure, I could stay up all night in a city. Always lit, always open, shops and bars provide something to do. But here, in the dark, there's nothing to stay up for besides the stars.

My Travelers sleep, clean and full of boiled fish, unmoving in the light of flickering fire. Beyond them, there's nothing. Just black water, black sky, black night-sounds.

That sound, though, was all wrong.

I know this world and how it feels. I know the tiny, cruel lapping of water on the shore, and the sound of my Travelers sleeping before tomorrow's hike.

I also know the sound of Sundered feet landing on a nearby tuft. It wasn't Gorish. He's sitting next to me, staring at his hands.

My heart beats faster. I concentrate, feeling for this new intruder. It's free. Unclaimed.

Two free ones in the same area? That never happens. Never. This has to be some kind of a trick, or a trap. But what kind could this possibly be?

Gorish starts to hum.

It's a tune I know, familiar from early school. *Fifth-tier's strong and lifts big blocks, not too bright but strong as ox. Fourth-tier's fine with clever fingers, painting, sculptures, make good singers....* It's catchy. Kids' tunes are.

Tiers indicate intelligence and power. It's a simple system, but Gorish isn't even fifth-tier. Nobody numbers Sundered Ones that low. There's no point. He has power, yeah, but not a lot—I doubt he could levitate anything heavy, or turn things into other, more useful things. He doesn't have the physical strength of fifth-tier, the delicate dexterity of fourth. The gentleness of third, or the feral viciousness of second. Or... whatever it is first-tiers have. I don't know. They weren't in the rhyme.

Gorish keeps humming. *Third-tier's quiet, good for play, safe for children every day. Second-tier's wild, feral, free, eats everyone, but works for me. Claim the rest with little work, but they die soon, so best not shirk.*

The fire crackles. *Thup-thup* go Sundered feet on a nearby tuft. Sundered Ones leap like fleas, and they never miss coming down, not even the stupid ones. I lick my lips. "Gorish."

Gorish looks up from the little suction cups on the ends of his fingers. "Yes, master?"

I feel my mind-fingers deep in his skull, filling those holes never meant for my thoughts. He has to answer me honestly. "Is there another Sundered One out there?"

His gaze is steady. "Always, master."

Yeah, not what I was asking, but okay. I might argue with it, honestly. There aren't enough Sundered by far—the best estimate puts their number at a few thousand, about the same as us, but shorter lifespans. "There's one very close now. Are there any people with him?" That's not specific enough. I need to be sure. "Is he claimed?"

"No, master! He is not!" Still crouched, he does a weird little shuffle, like he's celebrating that he gave me the right answer.

So the new Sundered is free. I'm not letting this chance pass me by. "Can he see us?"

Gorish sort of sniffs. "Oh, yes, master. He's quite close. He's superior!"

"He's high-tier?"

"Yes, master!"

Oh, wow. Third-tier, I can claim, and he'd be worth the risk. A hundred Gorishes wouldn't fetch the kind of money a third-tier would—but if he's second-tier, I'll have a struggle on my hands.

They're violent, hard to claim. He could pull a reversal, kill me, and get away. Is it worth it? Is he worth the risk?

I'll hate myself if I don't try. "Which way is he, Gorish?"

"He's—" Gorish stops and blinks. *Thup-thup* sounds to my left, and Gorish points and whispers. "He's looking at us, master."

I bet he is. Well, little guy, your curiosity just cost you your freedom. I reach out with my mind and my will, trying to find that oddly incomplete sense of a Sundered One in the dark. Emptiness, heat, everything moist and muddy and alone—

Light jolts through my eyes, and everything spins.

Gorish stops me from falling, catching my waist with his suction-cup hands, but my head is coming off, I swear my head is coming *off*, and if he lets go I'll fall in the water, but if I don't let go of him I can't hold on to this new huge mind.

And it's huge, holes big enough to swallow and lose me, angles too sharp to touch without cutting, taste too foreign to fully know. First-tier? Has to be first-tier because he's too different from third to be second, and I cry out, shouting, screaming, twisting in Gorish's grip—

More shouts join mine, and more people grip me to pull me backwards because *I am trying to hurl myself into the water to get closer to that mind.*

No, no, he's made me insane! "NO!" Can't hold them both— "Somebody claim him!" I scream and loose Gorish with a flick of my mental wrist, and he makes all of one hop on his own before someone else claims him.

This new huge mind and I wrestle, but now, without distraction, he's mine.

I am whole. He is not.

Gripping where there is no grip, fighting where my will batters his, and he's losing now, losing. I fly up out of the dark as his empty spaces conform to me.

Mine. You are mine!

Suddenly, I'm back in my skin, kneeling in the mud, dripping with sweat and blinking white spots away from my eyes. It seems so much quieter, even though people are still shouting.

Don't care.

Come to me, Sundered One.

Come to me.

He lands in front of me with grace like gravity doesn't matter and a shape I've never seen, so human that if he weren't flawless ebony black and eerily lovely I might be fooled. His hair is long and straight, the same black as his skin, and his irises burn bright orange. Sundered always go naked unless we force them clothed, but not him: he wears a short white kilt slung low and loose on his hips. "My lord." His voice is young like mine, barely into adulthood. Like a human servant, he kneels.

First-tier. I caught a first-tier. Ung—my head is so heavy it's going to fall off my neck.

Gorish makes worried noises. My Travelers demand answers, shouting in the confusion. I can't answer yet. I can't take my eyes off him. I've bagged a first-tier Sundered. From now on, everything in my world is changed.

2 AAKESH

My Sundered is a perfect point of stillness in the eye of a storm. He doesn't move, but his mind isn't settled around mine. It shifts against me, claimed, but not calm.

I might not be able to hold him.

"Harry!" Demos grips my shoulder, shakes me. "Storm!"

What?

Thunder booms in the distance.

No. I struggle to function, to beat the dizziness, the fuzziness.

Demos' eyes are wide, and sweat slides down his shaved head toward the mud. "Harry!"

Thunder means rain and slick mud and sinking boats. "Up," I croak, and discover I'm hoarse from shouting. "Get everybody up and packed. Direction?"

"It's coming from the south-west," Demos says. "We're already packing. Harry, what the hell just happened?"

I'm the leader. Their safety is on me. We have to move before the rain gets here. "Later! No time now, go, go!"

His jaw tightens, but he obeys.

I can't stand.

My fists dent the mud. My body rocks in time with my straining heart, making my breathing stutter. Stand, Harry. I have to stand.

Wet footsteps, shouts, the low thunks of tools thrown into boats. Stand, Harry, before they think you need help! Lead! *Lead*!

"My lord." My new Sundered crouches there, not smiling like Gorish, watching me with unblinking orange eyes.

He's first-tier. What can they do? How much power does he have? "What?" I manage between clenched teeth.

"My name is Aakesh."

I didn't ask him his name.

We stare at each other, this Sundered who volunteered his name and me unable to think. That mind moves around mine, unhappy with my intrusion. He's barely a few feet from me, and I'm on the edge of the water. He could send me in there if he gets control with a reversal. I'd be killed before anyone even knew I was gone.

I have to hold him. "Aakesh," I bark, forcing my throat to work. "You may not bring harm to me and my Travelers, do you understand? You're mine. No harm! That's an order!"

I may have gotten a little loud. My Travelers stare at me, backlit by the weirdness of storm-light.

Aakesh nods regally, like he's a king granting a favor. "Understood, my lord."

What the hell have I claimed?

"Harry, we've got to get moving!" Demos shouts, and lightning strikes in the distance. White-purple threads dance over the water.

Son of a bitch, don't think about Aakesh now. Stand, Harry! Stand!

I overbalance. My head is too heavy. I stagger, and then I fall.

I fall toward the water.

I don't have time to scream. Something like a log slams into my midsection and lifts me, flings me, and the world goes upside down. I flip upside-down, take one strained gasp—and suddenly, I'm in my boat. Just *there*, paddle in my lap like nothing happened, bobbing up and down with the storm-bred current.

Aakesh is on the tufts a few feet away, looking at me with those orange eyes while his hair settles down around him like gossamer threads.

I stare back at him, my hands shaking.

"Harry, come on!" shouts somebody, I don't even know who, and I realize they're all pulling away from me. Paddling, moving, not waiting for the storm to catch them.

I stare at Aakesh a moment more before pushing off after the others. I have to catch them. Overtake them. I have to lead.

Aakesh saved me.

I didn't tell him to. He applied what I said, found connotations in my order. He interpreted. Sundered don't do that, their broken minds don't do that. How did he do that?

My hands are still shaking.

It's deadly-dark once we're away from the fire. If there are islands or tufts or anything else that might knock us out of our boats, we won't know it until it's too late. Rain starts to fall, lightly for now, mingling with my sweat. My back strains and heaves as I pull ahead, passing the others, finally sliding past Tomas and Demos' brotherly two-seater and into the lead. It's my job to take the risk. If I flounder, they'll know not to follow me.

Movement catches my eye, something impossibly dark against the gloom: Aakesh. He moves ahead of us like he's dancing, flying from tuft to tuft, just close enough that I can see his hair falling around him like whispers.

Realization numbs me: his jumps are telling me where not to go. Where there's land for his feet, there's land to capsize my boat. I didn't command him to do that. I didn't even think of it.

"Master!" says Gorish, bobbing alongside my boat, unbothered by the storm.

Keep paddling, keep going, row, row, row. "Hi. What?"

Gorish swims along, beaming up at me. "You're so nice," he says, and disappears back under the black water.

Huh?

Whatever, little guy. I have Travelers to lead.

The storm follows us, blowing around our perimeter and chasing us with death. Lightning explodes in the distance, leaping over the water like cracks in ice. Thunder echoes, and we row, nearly blind in the dark but for the silent guidance from my new Sundered One. I can't afford to question whether I can trust him.

My head stays too heavy, and my neck aches. A psychosomatic reaction. There's no physical weight in my head.

I still feel him.

Little by little, the rain slows down. Dawn tints the sky, washing away the storm. We've rowed the whole night, and the clouds are finally far behind us.

My arms, shoulders, and back hurt like I've been beaten. Did we all survive? Yeah—I see them all behind me. Demos and Tomas. Toddy and Sandra. Kaia, in a one-person skiff like mine. Jax and Sheldon. That's everybody.

Relief approaches, then recedes: we sailed in completely unexplored places last night. I don't even know where we are now. The Hope could have been there, or some clue to the Hope, and because it was dark, I missed it.

Could have. Might have.

Stop being paranoid, Harry. It's impractical to turn back, and your Travelers would doubt you. Focus on what's happening right now.

Aakesh looks stranger in the light of day, too dark to be anything but shadow come to life. Every movement is smooth, almost circular—like he's dancing to music only he hears, all the time. His long, slender fingers aren't like mine, even if they seem human. He watches me, unreadable.

"Aakesh." My voice sounds tired.

"This way to landfall, my lord."

I didn't ask him. He's anticipating, again. I'm suddenly cold. "How close are we to a city?"

"Six days' travel, my lord," he says, for once not answering before I've fully asked my question.

Wow. We made impossibly good time last night. "All right. Starting tomorrow, I want you to guide us there. No tricks. No one gets lost or dumped into the water."

He nods, turns, and hops, fine hair falling slowly behind him as he leads the way.

He interprets things. Anticipates. I've never heard of this in my life.

Focus, Harry. Once we reach landfall, we'll eat, then sleep. Everyone gets fruit, and we'll brew some tea. After a night like this, we deserve it.

Aakesh chose dry landfall, covered in crumbly dust instead of mud.

It's safe enough for me to take out my map.

I can't help feeling calm when I touch it, grounded, even anchored. The heavy parchment is thick and smooth against my fingers, and makes no sound as it unfolds. I prefer it to the thin, cheap paper that makes up books, exams, and bills of sale in the cities. Those things all fall apart within a couple years, but parchment lasts. Treated animal skin, it survives generations, utterly precious.

My sparse notes join my forefathers', marking broad expanses of emptiness with little black islands and big city dots. Carefully notated warnings indicate dangerous places, and angry red x's mark where the Hope of Humanity wasn't.

The Hope of Humanity is a myth, a legend. A panacea, maybe machine or maybe magic, or maybe just knowledge stored away for the future. It's connected to our wrecked Earth, showing up at the same time as the black water and the Sundered Ones in our history.

Nobody knows what it is. My family has searched for it for a long time, following hints of a story that claims the Hope can fix it all. It'll fix the water. Fix the Sundered. Fix us.

How or why doesn't matter. Questions aren't really encouraged among the Iskinder bloodline. We paddle the world, scavenging salvage, and looking for the Hope. It's what we do, what my father did, and what I do, and what my son will someday be expected to do, end of story.

It's not what I wanted to do. It doesn't matter. The Sundered are going extinct, and once they do, we will follow. Someone has to try, and nobody else believes.

A familiar funk of fish surrounds me. "What is it, Gorish?"

"You're nice. Won't forget, nice master," Gorish whispers.

That's the second time he's said something like that. I look up, tearing myself from the blots and squiggles on parchment. "What the hell are you talking about?"

"Nice," Gorish says, and he reaches out with his little suction-cup fingers as if to touch my face.

I stare at him.

He drops his hand. "Bye!" he squeaks, and bounces off.

What the hell was that about?

Aakesh crouches nearby, his toes teasingly in the first inch of black water, his orange eyes steadily locked on me. Gorish splashes over and squats behind him, deeper in the water, like a servant following him around or something. Now they're both staring at me.

Whatever.

"Harry," says Demos, and offers me an apple.

It's the most delicious thing I've ever had.

It's a mush apple. It's brown, and the skin's wrinkled, but it doesn't taste like mud or boiled fish. It tastes like bliss, and I know what that means: it means we've been out here long enough, and it's definitely time to get to the city.

Six days.

I'll find the Hope someday. I will. But I need my Travelers to do it, and my Travelers need a break. "Gorish, Aakesh. Gather the water." Time for a bath.

My head is heavy. My thoughts are slow. When we get to the city, I'm selling Aakesh at once. Someone who makes a living out of this kind of thing can have him, and I can get back to business.

"Master!" Gorish's voice slices through my skull, making it heavier even though he's not mine.

Who claimed him? Well, everybody. They keep handing him off to one another, practicing. Once we're out of school, most people never get the chance to claim Sundered. They're too valuable for anyone but politicians and people with money to have, so I can't blame my Travelers for playing around. I just don't want them getting too rough. "Kaia."

She stops in mid-laugh, Gorish dancing in front of her like a marionette. He ducks like he was caught doing something wrong.

I'm too tired to deal with childishness. "Kaia, just leave him alone. He's had a longer day than we have, okay? If you use him up, I'm taking it out of your cut."

She pouts, sticking out that lower lip of hers, but she obeys. I'm younger than she is, younger than most of them, but they still obey.

"So nice, master," Gorish says warmly enough to make it weird, and bounces into the water with a splash.

I'm not your master anymore, buddy. You really must be broken.

We make good time before landfall, and I almost swear I can see a faint outline of city walls in the distance. I even imagine I can smell it, impossible as that is. My own brain works against me.

I wonder which city this is. My guess is Danton, which I haven't been to before, but if it's anything like the cities in this region, it's ugly, nasty, and it stinks, but it's better than nothing.

One of these days, I have to choose a city to continue the family line. I'll take the few years necessary to make a baby, teach the baby how to read maps, and then leave the baby with my maps as I continue to explore. I'm just nineteen. I can put off heir-making a little longer, can't I? And who knows? If I find the Hope, I don't have to make one—or I don't have to look at family as continuing the legacy. I can have a family like a normal person. I can make a home.

I'm getting ahead of myself. There are too many blank spots on my map.

"You all right?" says Sandra quietly.

She has good timing. Her voice pulls me out of my gloom. "Yeah."

She nods, but I don't think she believes me.

Toddy bounces over to crouch next to her, his smile crooked and playful. He's fifteen. A baby. This is all still just a great adventure to him. "You sure you're okay, Harry? You don't look okay."

I bet I don't.

Aakesh crouches there with his toes in the water that would kill us. He's not doing that by accident. My claimed, leashed Sundered is mocking me.

"Harry?" Tod really sounds unsure.

"I'm okay, guys. Get to work with the others, okay? Help get the tents set up. You had a turn with Gorish yet?"

Toddy looks so happy. "Yeah! I did great!"

"Ugh, no," says Sandra, making a face.

No idea what her problem is. I can't help a little smile for Toddy. "He likes you?"

"Likes me?" Toddy looks so confused. "I don't know. Why?"

As if the Sundered can't like or dislike. As if they aren't alive.

Whatever. That's the school system's fault, not mine. "Hurry with the tents. We need to sleep soon."

"Yes, sir, Harry, sir!" Toddy says, and salutes just for fun. I salute back. It makes him happy. He goes away.

Sandra watches me a moment more, then leaves without a word. There's dried mud in her light hair.

My smile is heavy, heavy like my head, and it falls away. I need a break.

City, whatever you are, here we come.

On the third day, I can definitely see the city walls from my skiff.

That's impossible.

It was six days away. Aakesh said so.

My Travelers know something's wrong. They all wear the same spooked expression, though none of them say what's wrong out loud. We covered way more ground than we should. But we didn't do anything differently. We rowed. We slept. We ate. Aakesh showed us landfall each night.

We shouldn't be close enough to see the walls.

Did he lie to me about how far we were? He can't—and why would he, anyway? What's there to gain by that? So we wouldn't eat enough? So we'd push harder, row longer, and tire ourselves out?

This is stupid. I'm getting worked up over something I'm going to sell.

Still. The city's closer. Too close.

I don't like it when things don't make sense.

I can smell it before we arrive. Lucky us: it's going to be a typical equatorial city.

Because of the number of people and the way the walls are built, central-western cities have limited airflow. In years past, there were machines built into those walls to pump fresh air in and cycle old air out, but most of them have broken.

Nobody knows how they worked. Yet another technological wonder lost to our dying world.

This city has huge walls, reaching up into the sky in a nasty brown that never looks clean. There's no gate. There are Sundered Ones, claimed by people who hide in the towers, and those people get to decide who can enter. If you're allowed, the Sundered make a way. If you're not, they don't.

My Travelers are quiet, all too aware we got here in half the time we should. Together, we row toward the main tower, which juts from the water like a big ugly phallic symbol. The city's official Sundered Ones swarm through the windows to meet us, getting a good look at who we are.

They're mismatched, mostly fourth-tier and lower, and vaguely animalistic, though no one Sundered looks quite like another. I have no idea how their species developed. Some have fur and some don't. Some have scales, or lizard faces, or big hairy limbs. That one is purple with a pig snout, but his tail is long and clever. They all cling to the walls like spiders, like their "down" isn't the same as ours.

Some of them look like they've been claimed too long.

It's easy to tell. Their eyes go white, pupils disappeared, and they're slow to respond to orders. A couple of these guys are past that point, so gone I'm surprised they don't just die right here and fall into the water.

I can't believe the waste. This city is run by fools.

We're running out of Sundered Ones. Nobody knows how they reproduce. It's obvious which are male and which are female, but that doesn't seem to matter. Breeding them does nothing, and every generation, there are fewer Sundered to go around.

They can still be caught in the southern portions of this world, but every year, there are fewer found. Without them, we won't be able to eat. Without them, we won't be able to build. Everything will fall apart.

"Announce yourself!" shouts one of the guards, as if we don't know the real threat comes from the Sundered Ones clinging to the walls.

My name means something. People expect crazy but great things from my family. Crazy: searching the world, traversing the vast open spaces after some imaginary thing. Great: nobody scavenges quite as well as an Iskinder. We come up with saleable items nobody else can find, things everyone thought were long gone. "I am Harold Iskinder. We travel for the Hope, searching for the cure. We come to you with goods to trade and benefit for your city." Blah, blabitty, blah.

"Hold, Harold Iskinder."

Their Sundered scan us, trying to determine if we're a threat.

I let them. They're low-tier, all of them. I bet Aakesh could keep us safe from anything they could do. That's kind of a nice realization.

"Harold Iskinder, you are welcome in Danton!" announces the guard, and then the Sundered make a way.

They plunge their fingers into the wall, into material that was rock-hard a second ago, but now shivers like chilled fat. It wobbles, gapes, and parts, curtains like trembling flesh on either side.

We paddle through.

They close it behind us. It's solid again.

The smells and sounds of equatorial city-life engulf us: grease and burning food, filth and unwashed bodies. I don't know how anyone can stand it.

Everything in Danton is the same ugly brown. The walkways are separated by long, straight canals of black water, like arteries— dangerous, but there's no choice about that. A city that doesn't allow the passage of black water through it crumbles apart in less than a week. Buildings rip themselves to pieces, twisting and cracking until a canal of some kind is formed, and if the structure didn't survive, well, too bad. It's like the canals relieve some kind of pressure.

Danton was poorly planned. Flat-faced buildings on either side rise five stories high, gaping with square black window-eyes, the source of even more heat and smell. There's barely enough room to crab-walk past the poles and awnings that cover the doorways of shops, especially if you've brought goods to sell.

Men with spears wait along the loading areas of the canal, watching us unload our stuff. "It's late and the market's closed," one of them says. "Be needing a claim ticket?"

Like I'm leaving anything valuable in their care. "No, thanks. We'll be taking it to our rooms. Aakesh?"

He's behind the guards, posture-perfect and deathly quiet. "Yes, my lord?"

They jump. Those hardened bastards jump out of their skins, deeply startled he was there. That's odd—but satisfying. "We need something to carry our wares. Can you help?"

He actually bows.

He hasn't done that before. It's almost like he's showing off for the gua-

The canal shakes.

It's a low, quick tremble, terrifying in the way it makes the water move, and then comes a *thump*. A pause, just long enough for Tomas to start, "What the sh-"

Six narrow boxes rise out of the walkway, right through the ground like some kind of magic show.

They're glass and brass with elegant construction, corners ornate with brass scrolling that climbs the glass walls. They hover inches off the ground as if they were sitting on rails, and the ground is smooth beneath them.

I've never seen anything so beautiful in my life.

Everybody freezes, eyes huge, maybe ready to run. The guards stare at Aakesh.

If I can sound casual about this, I'll look like I knew it would happen. "Thank you, Aakesh," I say loudly, evenly, as if I do this every day. "All right, people, load 'em up. Tomorrow we sell."

Aakesh stands there, calm, perfect, elegant. Wow.

My Sundered did that. Mine. Maybe selling him is a dumb thing to do. Wow.

Demos is the first to move, and once he piles his salvage into the boxes, the others join him.

"Market's open in the morning," one of the guards mumbles, remembering his duty. He adjusts his skullcap, giving Aakesh sideways looks.

My orange-eyed Sundered doesn't seem to care. He watches me, almost effeminate in contrast with these hairy guys.

"Thank you, gentlemen. With me!" I like it when my voice does that—deep. Authoritative. A leader's voice.

The carts float along behind me as if tied to me with string, and the hardest part is pretending it doesn't feel like they're stalking.

Read more: <u>The Sundered</u>

About the Author

Indie author Ruthanne Reid writes about elves, aliens,
vampires, and space-travel with equal abandon.
She has a degree in piano performance she never uses, a
second (slightly better used) degree in Biblical
Science, and currently lives in Phoenix, where the nights
are glorious for the imagination. She is the
author of the series Among the Mythos, and churns out
free short stories every couple of months.
Something of a mad book-gifting fairy, she believes good
stories should be shared. Subscribe to her free
email newsletter for free books and more at
http://amongthemythos.com.

18453372R00064

Printed in Great Britain
by Amazon